MAKE A WISH, ANNA

JULIANA CHAN

Copyright 2024 Juliana Chan

The right of Juliana Chan to be identified as the Author of the Work has been asserted by her in accordance with the Copyright, Designs and Patents Act 1988.

First published in 2024 by JC Books Ltd
Print ISBN 978-1-0687710-0-2
E-book ISBN 978-1-0687710-1-9

Apart from any use permitted under UK copyright law, this publication may only be reproduced, stored, or transmitted, in any form, or by any means, with prior permission, in accordance with the terms of licences issued by the Copyright Licensing Agency.

All characters in this publication are fictitious and any resemblance to real persons, living or dead, is purely coincidental.

Edited by Lesley Jones
Proofread and formatted by Abbie Rutherford at Abbie Editorial
Cover designed by Caravelle Creates

This book is dedicated to my mother, husband, and daughter; thank you for your constant patience, understanding, and love. I couldn't have done this without you all by my side.

PROLOGUE

The darkness embraced the sky, decorating it with a sea of stars. The surroundings were quiet with only the voice of the wind that whipped through the leaves, whistling like a scary dream. The breeze lightly touched my back, and my body shivered. I looked up at the sparkling sky, hoping to see a shooting star.

'Hey, sweetie.'

I looked behind me. My mum and dad were holding a birthday cake, and the burning candle lit up the surroundings like a joyful ray of hope.

I screamed out my excitement. 'Mum! Dad!'

'Happy birthday, sweetie,' Dad said.

'Make a wish, Anna,' Mum said.

Looking at both of them, I thought about what I should wish for.

'Take your time.' Dad smiled.

I closed my eyes and put my palms together, wishing for my only desire.

CHAPTER ONE

'Hey, Chris! You're on next.' The high-pitched voice assaulted my ears while I was brushing the hair of the movie star, Chris Steward. I looked up and saw the PA of the TV show. I'd forgotten her name, but I remembered her from other events; her short red hair and that signature cat eyeliner were certainly recognisable. The pushed-up cleavage under the tight T-shirt was not something I would forget either. The only difference was probably that the spotty face was looking flawless and glowing. I wondered if she had laser facial treatments.

'You're up in two minutes.' She lifted the corners of her lips and threw a seductive smile to Chris as if I did not exist.

Chris nodded and returned a smile. 'Sure, Kim,' he said.

She gaped but relaxed to a smile after a few seconds. I guessed she was surprised Chris had remembered her name.

In this industry, you get to work with many people, and it was difficult to memorise every person's name from the film crew. But this never happened to Chris; he literally imprinted everyone's name. His acting was superb, no argument. But it was not his acting skills that had led him to where he was; his people skills were what gave him the crown.

I finished my job and gave Chris a gentle pat on his arm. This was my cue for letting him know I was done.

He turned to me as he said, 'Thanks, see you later.'

I nodded but glued my eyes on my make-up equipment; I did not want to look at him right now. Without further response, I started packing up my stuff.

'Anna?' Chris said.

Hearing him call my name forced me to look up but I didn't stop packing.

'Are you okay?' he asked with a sceptical look on his face.

'Sure! Why?'

'You seem...' He paused and glanced at the PA who was next to him as if figuring out whether to continue the conversation.

'Just go, you're late,' I said.

He kept his stare on me and clearly wanted to stay longer but that foxy PA grabbed his arm and pulled him out of the changing room.

I watched Chris, my boyfriend, leave my sight, and breathed a sigh of relief.

Can you imagine dating a celebrity? What would it be like? Exciting? Luxurious?

In reality, you have a complimentary closet to hide in and an unlimited chance to watch flirty scenes of him with other women, and the best part is the vast opportunity to act like a puppet going wherever the master wants you to go. Sounds great?

Didn't people say 'All you need is love'? Love is so powerful that it could overcome any barrier.

It's easy to say, but it's hard if you're the one in the game.

Chris and I had been dating for a year, in secret. He was a Hollywood movie star. That God-made face and well-built body got him onto the list of the top ten hottest actors in Hollywood. Every girl, woman or even man adored him and would kill to be part of his life. His girlfriend – me – was just an average girl, ordinary and capable of nothing but make-up and styling. Obviously, he was too good for me. So why did he pick me? I wondered.

When I joined the company, I was assigned as his temporary stylist. Apparently, he had fired dozens of stylists before me, so I was hired to see if I could fit in with him.

'I like your work.' My manager, Jane, gave me compliments as she flipped through my portfolio. 'I see you have over ten years of experience...' She smiled but seemed hesitant as if she was concerned about my work. 'Maybe you can handle Chris,' she mumbled.

Did she mean for me to hear that? *I can handle Chris.*

What type of person needed to be 'handled'? Annoying, a troubled customer, and yes, Chris was that troubled customer she was referring to.

★ ★ ★ ★

Two years ago

I knocked on the door.

A husky voice came from inside. 'Come in.'

Anxiety immediately took over my body. I didn't know whether it was because I would be meeting Chris Steward, the most popular movie star of the year, or that the low-pitched masculine voice had scrambled my mind.

'Come on, Anna,' I whispered to myself, 'don't be a pussy.' I took a quick, deep breath and walked into the room.

A man with short, dishevelled blond hair was sitting in front of the dressing table reading an inch-thick script. He was dressed casually in a white polo shirt and blue shorts. I walked closer to him, and his smooth skin caught my attention. He was not wearing any concealer or foundation, but his skin was as perfect as if it had been photoshopped. The glow on his cheeks was natural and stunning; I was dying to run my finger over his skin and feel that silky softness.

'Hi, I'm Anna, your new stylist.'

The man slowly looked up, and when our gazes locked, my breathing stopped. His green eyes sparkled like diamonds. Those full lips were soft, shut tight. His angular jawline was strong and masculine and every part of his face was symmetrical, perfect as if made by God.

'Hi.' He stood up as he spoke.

His wide shoulders slowly rose above my head. He was so tall that I barely reached his shoulders. That well-trained body wasn't hidden by his shirt. His arm muscles were almost tearing off his sleeves. His face, his features, and every part of his body were made for a Hollywood movie star.

'I'm Chris,' he said with a formal smile and reached for a handshake. As my fingertips touched his skin, a mild electric current passed through me. I bit my bottom lip to stop myself from squawking. I took a glimpse at him, but I saw no expression on his face.

His zero response had confused me. Was it a delusion or

did that tickling spark really happen and he was just pretending to feel nothing?

'So should we start?' I looked away to stop myself from drilling into this incident.

'Sure.' He returned to his seat. 'But don't overdo my make-up or hair,' he said in a flat tone without hesitation. Each word was spoken like an order.

Great, I see why he needs to be 'handled'.

'Okay, I'll just give you a gentle touch-up.'

I usually start with make-up and leave hair until last, but as soon as my foundation brush touched his cheek, the hostile comments began.

'Please don't put anything too tan or too thick on me.'

'Don't worry, Chris. Just trust me.' I looked in the mirror and it reflected his face which was full of caution.

'I'm not sure if you can be trusted yet.' His voice was cold – so cold that I started to wonder if Jane hated me. The stern look on his face could petrify a bear.

I calmed myself and put on a smile. 'No problem – you'll be sure after this brush shows its magic.' I held up the brush and waved it like a wand.

I guessed trying to act cute was useless because he gave no response at all.

He kept quiet, which was good because I like to work undisturbed. But the silence ended too soon. When I moved on to his eyebrows, he was back to giving orders.

'Not too thick. I don't want to look like Ted.' There was that cold voice again. But it was not the cold voice that caught my attention.

'Ted?' I asked.

'You've never watched that movie? Ted, the bear.'

Then I remembered the teddy bear in the movie with bushy eyebrows.

The image of Chris having those bushy eyebrows was hilarious, and it was very hard to stop myself from giggling.

'I don't find it funny.' Chris frowned.

I forced myself not to laugh but I couldn't hide my smile. 'Relax,' I said.

'No, I don't relax when I am working.'

'You're not working now, I am,' I said as I smoothed powder onto his brow.

He smirked. 'Glad that you know.'

My hands froze in the air for a second, but I pretended I hadn't heard and focused back on his face.

The next few minutes were peaceful until I started brushing his hair.

'About the hair,' he said.

Here we go again.

'I don't want any hair hanging on my forehead or my cheeks.'

'Okay, I'll brush it all back.' I faked a smile.

'Don't put on too much hair gel, it's hard to wash out.'

'Okay, not too much hair gel.'

'Hairspray too, and don't spray it on my face.'

'Okay, not too much spray and not on your face.' I looked into the mirror again and saw his glare.

'I hope you know what you're doing.' He seemed irritated by my response.

I gave him a sweet angelic smile. But I wanted to bark at him like an angry dog.

Of course, I know what I'm doing. I've been doing it for over ten years, and professionally. If you want to look good in front of the camera, shut the hell up or otherwise do it yourself, you arrogant pig!

Barking out all the hateful thoughts in my mind gave peace to my heart. And the best thing was, Chris didn't say anything further.

For the next thirty minutes, the room was silent. No more nasty words or evil stares as if he had read my mind.

After I finished all the make-up and styling, Chris looked in the mirror, turning his head to different angles to check the details. I waited, prepared for his insults.

'Good,' he said, 'you did what I asked.'

Can you imagine my surprise? I thought he was going to insult my work, my attitude, and be unpleasant to me. But 'Good'? Wow!

'Oh...' I felt embarrassed for thinking he was an arrogant pig. 'That's good. I'm glad you like my work.'

'Thank you,' he added. But unlike before, his voice was sincere.

My completion of his little *challenge* opened up the fast lane to our partnership. No nasty words or concerns from him in the following weeks; I guessed I had passed his test.

'So, what's your hobby?' Chris asked while he was driving. He likes to drive his own car to work to save time, and he was generous enough to let me come along free of charge.

That day I was his passenger again; we'd just finished a modelling job and were heading to a media interview.

'Nothing much. Sometimes I read.' I made something up to avoid giving too much detail.

I always felt as if I lived in a different world compared with the people I worked with, so I opted to keep my distance.

'What do you read?' he asked.

'Um...' I muttered, trying to think of something in three seconds.

It couldn't be books because I didn't even remember the last time I read a book. The only thing I read was those cheesy magazines.

Oh well.

'I like to read magazines,' I said, hoping this boring answer would stop him from questioning further.

'What kind?'

'Gossip,' I said.

'Interesting choice.' He smirked. 'Anything about me?'

'I guess so.' I gave a random answer, praying he would stop asking questions.

Chris narrowed his brow. 'You guess? I thought you'd been reading them?'

Damn. The truth was I never read the gossip column.

'Um...' I muttered again, trying to figure out a better answer.

Maybe tell him I check out the styling of celebrities, just don't mention...

'The sex column.' I said the last thing that had flashed through my mind, also the one that I shouldn't have said.

The sex column, the sex column, the sex column...

Those three words echoed in my ears like the morning alarm.

I did not say that out loud, did I?

Yes, you did, Anna. Yes, you did!

The air turned thin and my body temperature rose; my heart stopped, and my whole body froze. It appeared to me that I had just made a fool of myself.

Maybe he didn't hear that.

My eyes slowly slid to the side to peek at Chris. But he was unreadable, focusing only on driving.

For the next ten minutes, both of us were silent.

The car passed by one building after another until I saw the logo 'F/A' a couple of metres away. I knew we were almost there.

'Was it good?' Chris's deep smooth voice broke the silence.

I wasn't sure if I was fantasising, but the pitch of his husky voice sounded lower than usual, and the vibration created in the air travelled through my veins, short-circuited my brain and deprived me of my ability to think.

'What?' I could barely form a sentence, not to mention remember what I had said before.

He took a glance at me and returned his focus to the traffic. Slowly, he stopped at a traffic light and turned to me. His diamond-like eyes were glowing again, and an evil smile spread faintly across his face.

I looked at him and my heart jumped like a deer; the shortness of breath made me feel light-headed.

I think I need to call an ambulance right now.

'The sex column...' His eyes sparkled as he spoke. 'Was it good?' He grinned like a beautiful devil.

CHAPTER TWO

'We're all very excited about your next movie – it was shot in Europe, right?' the reporter asked.

'Yes, we went to Spain, Italy, and France.' Chris's eyes sparkled under the spotlights, attractive like a massive magnet, captivating the reporter who leaned closer to him every second.

Staring blankly at that perfect face, I thought about the last words he'd said to me today.

Was it good?

Just thinking of that evil grin made me flush.

I peeked at the clock, counting down to the last ten minutes of the interview. When it finally pointed to twelve, I wasted no time grabbing our coats; it was the end of the working day.

Thank God.

Chris came over and took his coat. 'Where next?'

'We're done for today.'

When we got out of the building, I prepared myself to sneak away like a thief.

'What are you doing tonight?' Chris asked before I could fade away.

'Huh?'

'Would you like to join me for dinner?' Chris smiled with half-closed eyes. His sensuality was still sexy but didn't raise my adrenaline as much as it had this afternoon.

I missed that evil smile, but the embarrassed conversation we'd had this afternoon wasn't something I wanted to remember again.

Was it good?

Those words flashed in my head and once again my face grew hot. I turned away to hide my burning cheeks.

'Are you okay?' Chris asked.

I nodded but kept my face looking away from him.

'Would you like to have sushi?' he asked.

I would like to run.

I scanned all the possible exits and finally glued my eyes at the bus stop on the opposite street.

'Probably not.' I began to move towards the bus stop. 'I'm more of a burger girl. Why don't you go to have sushi tonight, and I will see you...'

'All right, let's have a burger then,' Chris said and grabbed my wrist.

The sudden skin-on-skin sensation stapled my feet to the ground. 'What?' I widened my eyes and looked at Chris. He was staring at my cheeks, and slowly a smile appeared on his face and gradually broadened. I guessed my flushed face was the reason for that big smile.

'Stop smiling like a villain,' I said.

'I can't help it, your red face has made me hungry.' He laughed.

'What?' I wanted to punch myself for that shaky voice. His words had made my heart bump like a galloping horse.

We kept our gazes on each other and neither of us looked away.

'Just joking.' He put away his evil smile and ended the awkward moment. 'Come on, let's go and eat.' He went into his car before I could object, leaving me no choice but to follow.

Chris drove us to an area near our agency. He pulled over next to a restaurant one block away from our office. But it was more like a pub than a restaurant.

The place was filled with vintage wooden tables and chairs; old faded photos hung on the walls and the scent of oak floated in the air.

Without checking around, Chris grabbed the furthest table in the most private corner of the pub.

After we were seated, a mouth-watering sweet scent of onion and beef rose from every corner of the restaurant. It totally awoke my appetite.

'You do have friends!' A man with a strong Scottish accent came over wearing a smirk on his face. He wore a plain white shirt with a pair of black pants, nothing fancy or expensive. With his silver hair and the fine lines on his face, he looked to be in his fifties.

'Of course I have friends.' Chris smiled and shook hands with the man. 'This is my colleague, Anna.'

I shook hands with Richard after the short introduction.

'Richard is the owner of this place,' Chris said.

'This restaurant is amazing,' I said. 'Very classic.'

'Wait till the food comes.' Richard smiled.

Richard returned to the cash desk and a waiter came over to take our order.

'I'd like an Angus beef double cheeseburger with extra onion and mushrooms, plus skinny chips,' I said.

'Are you a burger expert?' Chris chuckled.

'I am no expert, but I do have a special preference for burgers.'

The waiter soon served us food and beer.

I poured a pint of beer down my throat before I even started my meal.

'Slow down, or you'll choke yourself.' Chris arched his brows, looking concerned.

'I haven't drunk beer for a very long time. It felt good.' I burped to show my satisfaction. But perhaps I shouldn't have drunk so much before eating; the alcohol seeped into my brain, slowing down my thoughts. I even felt the heat rising on my cheeks.

'You drank too much too fast,' Chris said. 'Have some food, it will make you feel better.'

I grabbed the burger and dived into the juicy beef heaven. The burger was scrumptious; the medium-rare beef was succulent without being greasy and perfectly paired with the mild-tasting cheese; the acidity in the tomato and crunchy lettuce awakened my mind.

'This is delicious!' I looked at Chris with a mouthful of burger.

Chris chuckled. 'I treated you to a burger, so in return, why don't you tell me about yourself,' Chris said and put a chip into his mouth.

'Sure, you go first.' I guessed the beer gave me the nerve to negotiate.

Chris chortled. 'What do you want to know?'

I forced my lagging brain to generate some insightful questions.

'Where do you live?' After ten seconds of *serious* thinking, I'd come up with this meaningful question.

Wonderful.

'West London,' he answered.

'You live with your parents?'

'No, I live with a friend.'

'Man or woman?'

Chris paused a second before answering. 'A man.'

It would have been a good idea to dig into this topic, but probing people was never my speciality, especially co-workers, so I decided to ask something else.

'How did you become such a great actor?' I asked.

Chris burst out laughing. 'Do you think I'm great?'

'Well, yeah, the guy named Oscar agreed with me too, right?'

Chris carried on laughing. 'I think my acting skills are quite standard and, to be honest, I don't think I am that talented. I'm just lucky to have a great teacher and opportunities.'

Chris's voice gradually sounded far and distant. 'You know, many people have more talent than me. But most of them can't make it to the stage. It's not because of looks or skill, it's all about chances.'

'Well, actually the looks matter.' I smiled.

'Oh, please.' Chris rolled his eyes. 'There are lots of beautiful people in Hollywood. Many are more attractive than me. You know this better than anyone.'

'True, Hollywood is filled with angels.' I turned my smile into an evil grin. 'But none as breathtaking as you.'

I regretted it the second I spilled those words.

Seriously, what's wrong with you, Anna? And don't blame it on the beer. Why are you flirting with Chris? He could fire you if he wanted. Oh no – does he think that I was flirting with him? But whatever he thinks, I better change the subject right now.

While my brain was debating the best way to change the subject, I calmly poured myself a glass of water to buy time.

After silently counting three, two, one, I looked up and shot a shiny smile at Chris to hide my agenda.

'Do you have any hobbies?' I tried to sound as natural as I could.

'Huh?' he said as he rested one elbow on the table with his face on his fist, looking calm.

I was relieved to see a peaceful look on his face.

'I mean, what do you like to do in your leisure time?' I hoped he didn't think that I was flirting with him. Actually, I hoped he had forgotten what I had said earlier.

'Tennis, skiing, surfing...' As he spoke, a mildly evil grin rose on his face. 'Any kind of sport.'

I didn't know why the devil flashed me an evil smile and my stupid brain was running too slow to figure it all out, so I ignored whatever signal he was giving me and carried on with my questions. 'Did you play for any school teams?'

'Nope. I spent most of the time at the drama club trying to memorise lines. You know, performing drama on stage is quite different from making a movie or TV show where you can pause at each scene. You need to remember literally every line before you go on stage.' He finished off his beer and quickly ordered another round for both of us.

'Besides,' he continued, 'I don't like to have the co-star waiting for me on stage.'

'What does it feel like to be on stage the first time?'

'Amazing,' he answered without thinking, no hesitation.

The spark in his eyes once again drew all my attention.

'I remember I was ten years old, a month after my

birthday. The play was on a small stage at the town hall. There wasn't much of an audience, but the most important people were there for me – my mum and dad, siblings, my friends from school and even some of the neighbours. They all came to see my horrible performance.' He laughed.

'Was it that bad?'

'Oh, it was awful. I forgot my lines, I forgot to leave the stage, my costume fell off, everything was a mess.' He chuckled. 'But whenever my performance made the audience laugh, all the difficulties seemed worth it.' He gave me a sheepish smile.

Through my work, I encountered hundreds of beautiful and talented people, but never had anyone given me goosebumps simply by talking about his past. The dazzle on him wasn't an act – it came naturally, and perhaps that's what made him a superstar.

This superstar had a beloved family and friends, he had the best childhood and a great life. Whereas I was just a speck of dust on earth, by chance having the luxury to look up to this sparkling star.

We had crossed paths because of our jobs, but our path ended when we were off work. We lived in totally different worlds.

Chris broke the silence. 'How about you? What was your childhood like?'

Immediately, my sadness and sense of inferiority took over.

'Nothing special. I was just a normal schoolgirl.' I forced out a smile and tried to back away from the topic.

'I'm sure you have more to tell,' Chris said.

'Well, what can I say? I just went to school, kept to myself.'

Our eyes locked for a second and I averted my gaze to block him from reading my mind.

'Anyway, thank you for your recommendation of this place,' I said. 'It's wonderful.'

'Glad you like it.'

'It's kind of late, we better get going. Our call time for tomorrow is at six in the morning.' I looked at the waiter and nodded to request the bill.

'Thank you,' Chris said.

'Why thank me?'

'Thank you for listening to my boring story.' He laughed.

'No, I love it, you have an extraordinary past,' I said with sincerity.

'Yeah,' he said. 'And one day you will tell me yours.'

I rolled my eyes to cover my sadness. 'I told you, I kept to myself. I was—'

'A normal schoolgirl,' he said.

We looked at each other and burst into laughter.

★ ★ ★ ★

I had been working with Chris for a couple of months; we'd got to know each other better and become closer.

As I knew him a bit more, I realised he was diligent and took everything related to work seriously. He was also a perfectionist, and would only deliver the best to the audience.

Though I always teased him for being too serious, I deeply respected and secretly admired him. He did not graduate with a performing arts degree, but he excelled at acting. I once saw him practising one line for over an hour just to get the accent and tone right. He was so immersed in his job that I seldom heard about his relationships.

One day, I passed by his changing room and witnessed him alone with the beautiful actress, Jennifer Caine.

Jennifer had her arms wrapped around Chris's waist and her body was leaning on his chest; she moved her head towards him and seemed about to plant her lips on his.

When I thought I was about to witness the hottest kiss, live, Chris stepped back and gently pushed her away.

Wow, that was a surprise.

I wanted to grab popcorn and stay for the next scene, but ethically it was not a good idea to peek at your work partner.

I quietly walked away from this unsolved mystery, but that did not stop my curiosity. The image of Chris rejecting such a beautiful woman was all I could think of. When I realised only the truth could unplug me from that scene, I put on my Sherlock hat and decided to become a one-day detective.

Throughout the day, I kept three feet away and secretly stared at Chris, searching for any possible reason that made him reject one of the sexiest women on earth. I watched him closely; whenever he made a move, my gaze followed.

I noticed he checked his phone during every break; was he messaging someone important? Sometimes, he even smiled at the phone. Maybe he had a girlfriend?

But it didn't take long for me to admit defeat; after all, my tiny brain was not made for being a detective. Or maybe I just needed to hire a work partner like Watson to help me dig deep into the evidence. After failing in a few attempts to sneak behind Chris to peek at his phone, I gave up.

Maybe it was not about my brain, it was about my

height. He was too tall and I couldn't peek behind his shoulder to see anything on his screen, end of story.

The day finished with our weekly meeting with Jane and, after that, Chris and I returned to his changing room to collect our belongings.

The changing room was empty, with only a huge mirror surrounded by light bulbs and a make-up desk on the side.

As I closed the door, Chris turned to me. 'Okay, what's wrong with you today?' He squinted and had both his hands on his hips. I guessed by his body language that my *secret* staring was not so secret after all.

I decided to play dumb. 'What do you mean?'

'You've been spying on me all day.'

'No, I haven't.'

'I know you were staring at me during the breaks.'

'No, I wasn't. Why would you think I was staring at you? You have eyes in the back of your head?' My last attempt to fool him.

'Just spit it out.' He crossed his arms on his chest.

I panicked and couldn't lock eyes with him. At the same time, my brain was spinning at supersonic speed trying to make something up. 'Fine, I think you're very attractive, so it was hard to look away.'

What a lunatic thing to say.

I guessed the answer was too lame. Chris burst out laughing.

When he finally calmed down, he took a quick scan of my face and before I could figure out what was on his mind, his eyes gradually filled with softness. 'Oh, honey.' He lowered his voice, making it sound smooth and sexy, but perhaps it was overdone because it gave me goosebumps.

Have you been to a haunted house at an amusement

park, and when you knew you were about to see the scary ghost, every nerve was so sensitive it gave you goosebumps? Right then, I had the feeling that I was about to meet the ghost.

'If you want me,' he said softly as he gently cupped my face in his hand, 'just ask.'

He lowered his head and his scent was so strong it made me light-headed. When his lips were about to touch mine, I used my remaining sense to push him away.

'Okay, okay, you win.' I held up my hands and surrendered.

Chris laughed and pulled himself out of character.

'So why are you spying on me?'

I confessed. 'I saw you with Jennifer.'

'And?' He looked confused as if he recalled nothing from today.

'And you pushed her away while she was trying to...' My tongue was tied at the weird moment; it was absurdly difficult to say the word 'Kiss'.

Chris frowned, perhaps trying to make sense of my words. But that lost expression didn't last long. I guess he had pieced it together.

'So?' He grinned.

'So?' I raised my voice. I couldn't believe what he just said. 'It was Jennifer Caine. *The* Jennifer Caine. She was listed in the top ten sexiest women alive. You don't push away a woman like that.'

'And your conclusion is?'

I whispered, 'You like men?'

Chris gaped and, for a second, I thought I'd got it right.

But the next second, he cackled so hard that it nearly split his sides. I felt like an idiot.

'What is so funny?' I frowned.

He calmed himself and stepped closer to me. 'Trust me, I love women more than you can imagine.' He lowered his head to my eye level. 'Or would you like to test me?' His lips slowly moved towards mine; each word he said was like a feather brushing my lips.

My heartbeat speeded up and I felt my cheeks flush. I stepped back and took a long breath. 'No need. I believe you.'

He burst into laughter again.

'So do you have a girlfriend?' I didn't know where the courage came from for me to ask Chris such a personal question.

Chris fell silent after he took a glance at me. I wondered if he felt uncomfortable with the question.

'Sorry, don't answer if you don't want to. Just asking in case she suddenly appears at our workspace and I can bring her to you.' I sent him a sheepish grin.

He still didn't reply, so I thought it was time to end the topic. I picked up my make-up case and prepared to leave the room. It had been a long day, and I was very tired.

Chris broke the silence. 'No, I don't have a girlfriend.'

I squinted, not buying his answer. 'Really? How come?'

'What do you mean by "How come"?'

'Come on, you know you're good-looking, how come you don't have a girlfriend?'

He pulled out his evil grin again. 'Do you want to be my girlfriend?'

Even though I understood he was just joking, those few words still raised my heartbeat; it was pounding so fast it was like a panicked horse running loose. I talked myself down to the reality that no way would a superstar want an ordinary-looking girlfriend like me.

I smiled to mask my crazy feelings; it was embarrassing enough to have those feelings to begin with, and it was best not to make it worse by having him think I had actually considered it for a second. 'Stop messing with me.' I gave him a useless punch on his arm. 'I've got to go. I'm so tired today.'

'I understand – being a detective is very tiring.' He grinned.

I turned my back on him and waved goodbye in the air.

After walking out of the room, I leaned on the door and took a long breath.

I rewound our conversation in my head and kept reminding myself that it was just a joke, I shouldn't be excited. I should remain calm and peaceful, but on the contrary – I felt thrilled and joyful. No matter how hard I tried, the smile stayed on my face for the rest of the day.

CHAPTER THREE

'Do you like barbecue?' Chris asked.

'Do you mean barbecue food or barbecue flavoured food?'

Chris sighed. 'Barbecue food, of course, you silly girl.'

I nodded; I couldn't care less. 'I guess so.'

'You don't know if you like barbecues?'

'Well...' I lowered my voice, feeling a bit embarrassed. 'I never had one, so I guess it's cool.'

'What? You never...' Chris paused as he saw my sheepish smile. 'Never mind. Do you want to try a barbecue?'

'Just you and me?'

'No – I'm going home tomorrow so I thought you might be interested in coming along.'

To meet his family? Was that okay or even professional? I mean, we weren't friends, we were just co-workers.

'It's just a casual gathering, don't overthink it,' Chris continued as I went silent. 'But if you...'

'Do I need to bring anything?' I asked.

'No.' A broad smile appeared on his face. 'Just bring yourself.'

The next day, Chris picked me up and drove us to his home, which was two hours away.

'Why have you brought a backpack? What's in it?'

'Oh.' I took out a bottle of whisky. 'I didn't want to come empty-handed, so I brought this.'

Chris took a glimpse at the name on the bottle. 'You've brought my family a seventeen-year-old Hibiki whisky?' He raised his voice and almost crashed the car. 'When did you buy that?'

I guess my puzzled face also confused him.

'How much was it?' Chris asked.

'Um...' I squinted to read the label on the bottle, trying to guess the price tag. 'A hundred pounds?'

Chris burst into laughter. 'This whisky costs over seven hundred.'

'Wow. That's pricey.'

'Yeah, so I guess you've been conned – it's a fake.'

'Don't worry,' I said firmly. 'I am pretty sure this is a real thing. It's a gift from a client.'

'Your client must be wealthy.'

'Yes. He's quite funny too. He gave this to me after I helped out at his sister's children's party.' The memory of children lining up for my service flashed into my head. 'Face painting,' I added.

'Keep the whisky for yourself,' Chris said.

'I don't drink whisky and it's just a waste sitting in my cupboard.'

Chris shook his head in disapproval but didn't argue further.

It was almost lunchtime when we arrived.

His family's house was located in a purely residential area surrounded by Colonial-style houses with rectangular gabled roofs, symmetrical windows, and earth-tone walls. This place looked very expensive.

A beautiful woman came up to us wearing a big smile. 'Oh, that's my boy,' she said. 'And he's brought a girl with him.' She flashed another big smile at me.

'Hi, Mum.' Chris gave his mum a big hug. 'This is Anna. Anna, this is Mum.'

'Call me Angela.' She hugged me. 'I can't wait to talk to you. Come.'

The interior of the house was stylish with minimal design; the contrast of the white painted walls and dark wooden floors created a calm and peaceful atmosphere. One long corridor was decorated with beautiful black-and-white photos hanging on the side, and everywhere the modern furniture highlighted the unique taste of the owner.

A handsome man walked towards us. 'You look taller. And you finally bring us a girl.'

Chris flushed. 'Stop it, you're embarrassing me.'

They gave each other a long hug. Then, the man switched his focus to me and introduced himself. He was Chris's father, Danny. I passed the whisky to Danny; he was so happy when he saw the bottle.

'That—'

'Don't ask!' Chris said. 'Just take it, all right.'

Danny said no more and gracefully accepted the bottle.

We walked out of the house to their garden, which was huge, probably twice the size of their house. A few men stood next to the barbecue and some women were preparing cocktails. Children were playing in a small play area in the corner.

'Are they all related to you?' I raised my eyebrows.

'Yep.' Chris smiled. 'Those three men next to the barbecue are my older brothers. That girl with the ponytail is my big sister, and the other three are my brothers' wives. That little boy is Ben, he's Joe's son. Those two girls are twins – Emma and Bonnie – they're Jim's daughters.'

As I watched them, a horrible sense of envy came out of nowhere. I bit my lip to swallow down my bitterness. 'You have a big family,' I said with a smile to cover my emotions.

'There's nothing to be happy about.' Chris laughed. 'Trust me, they can turn your life to hell,' Chris said as he walked towards them.

I watched the brothers greet each other, laughing and joking. The familiar feeling of loneliness and alienation slowly built in me. It was like watching people eating chicken in a commercial, showing you how good it was but, after all, it was only a visual sensation.

Chris's sister patted me gently. 'Would you like an appetiser?'

I was caught by surprise and felt as if I'd suddenly lost the ability to talk. I looked at the marinated BBQ chicken; the honey colour brightened my heart and pulled me back into the real world. I took a piece to embrace the mixture of smoky and sweet flavour.

'I'm Claire, by the way, Chris's big sis.'

Before I could say anything, someone shouted to me.

'Anna,' Chris squealed as he rushed toward us, 'don't tell her anything – she likes to dig my dirt.'

'What kind of dirt are we talking about?' Claire laughed.

Chris rolled his eyes and pulled me away from Claire. 'Let me introduce you to my brothers.'

Chris's brothers were tall, handsome and muscular,

especially his big brother John. He was a gym instructor. His second brother Jim was an accountant and his third brother Joe was a photographer.

'John, Jim, Joe.' I shot a gaze at Chris. 'Did you change your name?'

'No,' Jim said, 'he's just too annoying so Dad decided he doesn't belong to the J family.'

Chris laughed. 'So you think you're an angel?'

'All of you are troublesome!' Chris's dad showed up, smiling. 'Come on, guys. Lunch is ready.'

The round dining table was filled with amazing-looking gourmet food and wine. We sat in a circle and enjoyed our relaxing lunch.

'So how do you know each other?' Danny asked.

Chris and I exchanged a glance.

'We work together – she's my make-up artist,' Chris answered.

'Remember to share some beauty tips.' Claire shot me an admiring glance.

Out of nowhere, the voice of a young boy interrupted our conversation.

'Do you guys kiss at work?'

All of us immediately turned to the source of the voice; it was Joe's six-year-old son.

'Ben!' Joe's wife said, raising her voice. 'Who taught you that?'

'My friend Judy told me people kiss at work.'

'I'm sure your friend is wrong.' Joe patted his shiny little blond head.

'Really?' Ben looked up with his huge blue eyes. 'But last week she kissed me at prep time and said people do that all the time.'

Everyone burst into laughter.

'You've got yourself a girlfriend already!' Jim laughed and squeezed Ben's chubby cheek.

'Seems like Ben did better than you.' Danny shot a look at Chris, laughing out loud. 'You two are just workmates?'

'Dad!' Chris sighed.

'Yes.' I gave them a sheepish smile. 'Just workmates.'

Claire lowered her voice and asked, 'Do you know if he has a girlfriend?'

'I'm not sure.' I chuckled and shrugged.

'I don't think any girl could cope with him,' Claire said.

'You know I can hear your conversation?' Chris rolled his eyes.

'And you?' Angela asked me. 'Do you have a boyfriend?'

I laughed. 'No,' I said while glancing at Chris.

It might have been my delusion, but there was a glisten in his eyes when I admitted to not having a boyfriend; he seemed genuinely happy.

'Anna,' Joe said as he pointed to Chris, 'don't be fooled by his look. He's a very nice guy.'

'Okay, what do you mean by that?' Chris frowned and started arguing with Joe. Soon, John and Jim joined in the fight. The funny scene made me smile.

'So do you have any brothers or sisters?' Danny asked.

As if he was a king who had just made an announcement, everyone quieted down. I tried to act normal because I wasn't comfortable being under the spotlight.

'Um,' I mumbled, feeling slightly anxious, 'no.'

'You're an only child!' Jim said. 'Lucky you, you don't need to use second-hand stuff.'

I didn't want to correct him because my answer would

probably cause misery and pollute the vibe. So in the end, I just threw him a shy grin.

Although I thought they were no longer interested in my personal life, Danny seemed intrigued to know more about me.

'So do your parents live in London too?' Danny asked.

'Stop harassing my friend, Dad.' Chris frowned but smiled.

'I'm just asking your friend a simple question.' Danny chuckled.

'It's fine.' I forced a smile because I knew exactly how they would feel after I revealed the truth. 'My parents passed away when I was young.'

Immediately, the air clotted and the atmosphere fell silent. If you don't know how to kill a party, watch me.

After a weird, long silence, someone finally spoke.

'I'm very sorry to hear that,' Danny said.

Angela walked over to hug me. 'I'm sorry for your loss.'

I glanced at Chris, and he was gaping. My answer seemed to have detonated a bomb in his head.

While everyone looked sad and felt sorry, I brought up the lines I had practised many times. 'Don't worry.' I smiled. 'I believe one day a giant will come and take me to magic school.'

I guessed my lousy joke did the trick. As if nothing had happened, they all fell into laughter.

I looked at Chris; he forced a smile and was silent throughout lunch.

Apart from this little incident, the lunch went smoothly and was fun.

I followed Chris to his car as we prepared to leave.

Angela came over and passed me a box. 'Anna, take some chicken home – you're too skinny.' She smiled.

The chicken was still warm in the container, and the warmth travelled through my body to my heart.

Danny and the brothers also came over to say goodbye, and their kids waved at us until we were out of sight.

'Thank you, Chris,' I said. 'Your family was so friendly and the food was great.'

I took a peek at him, but his blank eyes and tightened lips were unreadable. I decided to keep quiet and thank him again later.

We went on the motorway, and the journey was long and boring. I struggled with whether I should turn on the radio because the silence had been hovering in the car for an hour.

When I lifted my hand to the radio, Chris broke the silence. 'Do you need to go home now? Can you go somewhere with me?'

'Sure, but where?'

'Just someplace where I can think.'

I nodded and he changed the route on the Google map.

Half an hour later, we arrived at a rooftop bar on the thirtieth floor of a commercial building. The waitress led us to a private corner and served us mocktails.

'Whenever I need to think, I come up here,' Chris said.

I looked up; the sun was still hanging in the boundless sky, but the orange shade suggested it would soon be hiding under nightfall. I took a sip of my drink and closed my eyes, grabbing the last chance to chill in the daylight with warm air touching my skin.

'You never told me,' Chris said eventually.

I glanced at him but didn't know what to say. I knew what he was referring to but I didn't have an answer for him.

My childhood was history. I never visited it or talked about it. For the sake of myself, I buried it in the deepest recess of my mind, because it ripped my heart apart every time I returned to that dark past.

So, whatever I felt, it stayed in my heart.

'It's not important.' I shrugged.

People with happy families would never understand my difficulties if I brought up the past. Just thinking of it, tears would spontaneously appear, followed by weeping and crying. I have done enough of that in my life and was sick of that emotional ride. Years of practice meant I had closed myself up; was that a good thing? Of course not, but if it could keep me away from tears, I didn't mind becoming a forever introvert.

The absence of sound attracted my attention. I looked at Chris and realised his gaze had been locked on me all this time. The olive-green eyes stared at me with gentle care, as if he was stroking my hair, patting my shoulder, offering the warmest hug to me. Remember a time when you were trying to hold back your tears and someone came over and simply said, 'Are you okay?' Just a simple sentence could make you burst into tears. He didn't need to speak; just by looking at me with those tender eyes, it could slowly tear up my disguise, leading me to fall into the darkness in a second. The overwhelming care heated my face, moistened my eyes. I broke off our eye contact and looked out to the sunset, hoping to calm my thundering mind. I steadied my vision and when I could finally hold on to my emotions, I forced a smile, giving myself the courage to finish the conversation.

'It was a long time ago. I hardly remember anything.' I tried to sound cold and distant, hoping he got the signal and played ball. Because I knew this was the last moment I could hold off the tears. A girl crying in public would draw attention and I was sure Chris did not want that.

After a long pause, Chris put on a smile, casually leaned back and returned his gaze to the sunset. 'Okay,' he said.

I secretly let out a long breath and was relieved that he'd finally dropped the topic, glad that he was a good team player; he always knew what to do and when to stop.

My depressive emotions gradually wore away, just like the sunset in the sky.

'So what kind of thinking do you do here?' I asked casually, trying to clear the tension between us.

'Lots of things,' he said, 'mostly about work and the scripts.'

'The scripts?'

'Yes, I take lots of time to think about the characters, about their lines, creating their unique gestures in my head.'

'Can't you just do that at home?'

Chris peeked at me and sent me a sheepish smile. 'Well, my roommate can be quite distracting. He likes to sing.'

'Is he good?'

'Well...' Chris paused. 'Would you like to hear him?'

'Sure.'

'Okay, let's go.'

'What? Now?'

'Yes, why not.'

This spontaneous plan sounded fun to me; it also took my attention away from that depressing moment of today.

So off we went, heading to Chris's house.

Modern and huge were the words to describe his penthouse. The view was amazing, the world at your feet, and all those lights decorating the surroundings.

A cold slippery touch nudged my lower leg. I looked

down and was welcomed by large black eyes. A big furry Samoyed was sniffing my ankle, and I kept still to watch him explore a human leg. When he noticed my observation, he paused and put a smile on his face.

Chris walked over with wine. 'This is Snowball.'

'He is your roommate?' I laughed.

'Yep, my best roommate,' he said.

I leaned over and gave Snowball a big hug. His thick fur was like a soft pillow inviting me to lie on top. He smelled like bubblegum; I guessed the groomer gave him that scent of shampoo.

'Let's sit.'

I sat on a white sofa, and Snowball rushed up and sat by my side. He laid his head on my lap, looking innocent. I could not stop petting him, his fur was so soft.

Chris came over to the sofa and sat next to me. While he passed me the wine, Snowball leaned over as if he wanted to take a sip.

'Nope,' Chris said.

Snowball howled like a wolf to indicate his disappointment.

'Okay, that's his way of telling me to piss off.' Chris laughed.

After a minute of arguing, Snowball finally calmed down when Chris gave him a treat.

'I see why you can't do your thinking here.' I laughed.

Chris quietly stared at me, but I guess he felt his gaze made me nervous, and he gently pulled away and looked at Snowball instead.

'Do you have a dog?' he asked.

'Nope.' I felt relief from his simple question. There was too much tension between us today.

'Why not?'

'It's too much of a responsibility and I don't spend a lot of time at home.'

A long and awkward silence took place again. When I was about to speak, probably some nonsense again, he asked, 'So you don't read your magazines at home?'

At first, I was confused by his question. Soon I realised he was referring to the lie I told him when we'd first met. I burst out laughing.

'Why are you laughing?' he questioned with a confused face, looking innocent.

'Fine, I made that up, okay!' I rolled my eyes and gave up trying to cover my lies. 'Stop bringing that up.'

The next second, Chris could not keep a straight face and blasted into laughter. He said, 'You know, at the time I thought it was a sex invitation.'

'What? No!' I screamed. My face turned hot just hearing the word 'sex' from his mouth. 'That's not how I'd do it.'

Chris calmed himself and pulled on an evil grin. 'So how would you do it?'

'What?' Damn that evil grin. It blanked out my mind again.

He leaned closer, and the scent of his mild cologne awakened my nerves. His breath was like a feather stroking my skin; the closer he got, the warmer I felt. Something was wrong with me.

'How?' he asked.

'How what?' I felt we were too close, so I unconsciously placed my hand on his chest to part our bodies. I tried to softly push him away, but he was solid as a rock.

'Sex...' he mumbled.

The word 'sex' almost gave me a heart attack again. I

looked up and met his eyes. He was smiling, staring at me with an affectionate glimmer.

'How do you give sex invitations?' he said softly into my ear.

'I...' I muttered. He was like a wizard and had just cast a spell on me. My mind blanked out like a broken computer.

Chris stared into my eyes, but in just a second he pulled away.

'Just messing with you.' He chuckled.

When he finally left my personal space, my energy bounced back. I took a deep breath and tried to breathe out the heat flowing through my veins.

'Don't make stuff up anymore, okay?' he said.

'Why?' I asked. His request was a bit weird. We were only work partners; no rules said we needed to tell each other everything.

He sank into silence, like the silence before a storm. 'Because I want to know you,' he said.

CHAPTER FOUR

Because I want to know you.

I woke up and the first thing that came to my mind was those six words.

That sentence was like a ghost. It had followed me home and appeared in my dream.

He was joking, right? He was a Hollywood star, and I was a small potato with ordinary looks. Who would want to know me? Not even myself. Come on, he was joking, right?

'Coffee?' Chris passed me a branded cup when I got into his car later that morning.

'Yes, I would love that.' I graciously accepted this morning's brain drink.

It would be a long drive today, and after yesterday's awkward moment, trapping myself in this small space with him made me fret. But in the end, it was a waste of time worrying about the unknown future. My manager kept me on the phone for nearly half of the trip, giving me a brief on Chris's new jobs.

'What did she want?' Chris asked after I hung up the phone.

'Just to tell me about your new movies and interviews.'

'Boring!' He laughed.

'Well, I've got news that you might be intrigued by...' I lifted a corner of my lips.

Chris shot me a glance after I went silent. 'You have three seconds to speak before I kick you out of the car.'

'Do you know you will be meeting Jennifer Caine today at the costume fitting?' I asked while I examined his face.

'Yeah. So Detective Anna will be busy today, huh?' Chris grinned but kept his eyes on the road.

I gave him a dry laugh.

Everything seemed fine, nothing had changed. I was glad we had returned to our work partner status. While Chris was driving I sneaked a look at his strong, masculine facial features; every angle was perfectly photo-ready. But the thought of this beautiful man talking to Jennifer Caine made me feel sick, and bitter and sour feelings rose from nowhere.

Even though my mood was absurd, the day was great. I was happy to see other make-up artists and the crew was nice; it was wonderful, apart from seeing Jennifer all over Chris the whole day. She just wouldn't stop shadowing him. But the worst part was Chris never asked her to get the hell out. Well, I get that he couldn't just tell her to piss off because they were work partners. But my anger was burning from inside.

'You got yourself a little fan,' I said as I got in his car.

Chris shot me a confused look but quickly realised who I was referring to. He burst into laughter. 'So what evidence did Detective Anna gather today?' He even lowered his voice to mimic an old-fashioned detective.

'Ms Caine is your big fan and you like her.' I lifted my face, concluding with confidence, but beneath that proud exterior I was full of sarcasm and anger.

'Do I?' He chuckled.

'Do you not?'

He didn't agree or deny.

After a busy week, I finally got two consecutive days off.

I cleaned the kitchen, mopped the floor, and got ready to go out for groceries. As I finished dressing and got out my grocery bag, my phone buzzed.

'What are you doing today?' The voice on the other end of the phone was smooth and deep and almost gave me a heart attack.

'Supermarket. Why?' I squeezed my fist to calm myself – he was intruding on my peaceful weekend.

'Do you need a lift?'

'Sounds great.' *Hell no.* 'But I'm heading out now so maybe next time...'

'Great, I'm right outside your house.' The voice sounded excited.

My phone almost fell out of my hand, and I grabbed it quickly. 'What?' I raised my voice.

Walking out of the house, I saw a familiar black Porsche, the one that picked me up for work every day. The tint on the windows shielded my visibility of the driver, but he flashed the car lights as if waving hello.

I walked over to the driver's side and he lowered the window as I leaned down.

I squinted. 'Why are you outside my house?'

'I was just driving through the neighbourhood and thought I'd see if you want company.' Chris seemed to have ignored my surprise and smiled casually.

'Well, I'm just going to the supermarket, if you want to come.'

'I would love to go to the supermarket with you.' His eyes sparkled with excitement. But quickly, I turned it into disappointment.

I held up my palm to him. 'No, you are going to sit in the car and wait for me,' I demanded. The thought of him being in a supermarket with half the customers ogling him was horrific. I doubted he could get out of there in one piece.

'Fine.' His voice dropped like an unhappy child's. 'Please be quick though.'

'Of course.' I got in the car and smiled at him. 'I will be quick because it's illegal to leave children in a car.'

'Shut up.' He burst out laughing and the next second, we were on our way to the supermarket.

After nearly an hour of shopping, well, more like battling for food in the supermarket like it was the end of the world, I returned to Chris's car with a huge bag of groceries.

'Did you buy an elephant? What took you so long?' he asked.

'I should have come here a bit earlier. There wasn't much food left in there. I actually had to fight for this last broccoli.' I held up a green plant that was only half the original size to show my victory.

'Is this a new type of broccoli? There are no buds?' Chris laughed.

'Yeah.' I snorted. 'Laugh all you want.' I rolled my receipt into a paper ball and threw it at him. 'If this is all they have, then I'll take it. Why? Because I'm skint and I don't have a choice.' I sighed and leaned back into the seat. 'How do you buy groceries, by the way? You can't just walk into a supermarket like me, right?'

Chris opened his mouth but no words came out.

'What's wrong?' I asked.

'Nothing.' He shut his mouth and turned away.

My Sherlock instinct told me he was hiding something. I squinted to study his face carefully and rewound the conversation we had just had. When I thought of one possible yet unimaginable answer, my eyes almost popped out.

'Oh my God!' My mouth opened wide and my jaw dropped to my chest. 'Don't tell me you have a butler to buy your groceries.'

Chris ignored my question and started the engine.

'Not a butler?' I raised one brow. 'Who is it?'

Chris took a breath and looked at me with red cheeks; only one person could have been the cause of that embarrassed expression.

'Your mum?' I almost screamed out my answer.

Chris shared the cutest sheepish smile ever. 'Yes, one point to Sherlock Anna.'

'What? You still need your mum to buy your groceries?' I raised my voice.

'She just orders it online for me.' He looked down to his lap and lowered his voice. 'My strength is not in online shopping.'

He flashed me another sheepish smile and scratched his head like a little boy.

This rare embarrassed look was cute enough for me to risk my career and take an unauthorised photo of him.

On the way home, I secretly peeked at Chris. Knowing that I might be one of the few who knew this side of him, my heart pounded faster, and my lips subconsciously twisted to a smile.

'Why are you smiling?' Chris took a glance at me and asked.

I should have been nervous about getting caught, but without knowing where my courage came from, I locked my gaze with his and broadened my smile.

'Would you like to learn online shopping?' I asked.

Chris huffed a laughed. 'You are joking.'

'Come up and find out.' I pointed to my house. 'I have all the equipment you need, except for money.'

Chris continued laughing, and when he saw the determination in my eyes, he quietened down. 'Are you sure?'

'Why? You scared?' I laughed. 'I don't bite. But you need to help me bring the groceries up.'

'Oh, I see why you offered the computer lesson.' Chris laughed. 'You need a delivery man.'

I rolled my eyes and threw a tissue at him.

⋆ ⋆ ⋆ ⋆

Chris Steward is at my house!

Chris Steward is at my house!

Chris Steward is at my house!

I was pretty sure if any girl had the same moment as I was having now, they would definitely post a message on their social media. But unlike them, I was the girl who got to see Chris Steward every single day; his visit should have made no damn difference to me.

At least that was what I thought.

I realised how wrong I was right after the door shut.

It suddenly dawned on me that I would be trapped in my five-hundred-square-foot tiny flat alone with him, and my heart rate rocketed sharply.

My heart was pounding, my head spinning and my blood pressure going up all at once. My weird brain even tried to enhance the effect by creating slow-motion footage of Chris walking out of my steamy bathroom half-naked with a towel around his waist, pushing back his dripping wet hair and locking his eyes on me as he slowly dropped the towel onto the floor.

At this point I admired my imagination; it had never been more creative.

'Are you okay?' Chris came out from the bathroom – fully dressed, of course.

'Yep.' I nodded.

'Why are you still holding a carrot?' He squinted.

'Huh?'

'You were holding the same carrot before I went to the bathroom.' He laughed. 'Something special about it?'

My weirdness had once again made a fool of me. I quickly put away the carrot and other groceries to avoid the reappearance of my silliness.

Chris sat on the sofa and scanned my flat.

My apartment was a small studio with nothing much in it. I kept my belongings to a minimum because I moved around a lot. A sofa, a double bed, a small open-plan kitchen, a bathroom and simple furniture.

'Where's your stuff?' Chris asked.

'This is my stuff.'

'There's nothing here.'

'What did you expect?'

'No pictures? Clothes?'

He pointed at my shoe tray. 'You have two pairs of shoes?'

I ignored his questions and took out my MacBook.

'Stopped being nosy and focus on your problem.' I typed in my password to start the computer and quickly navigated to a shopping site. 'Do you have an account?'

'Nope.'

'Okay, let's get you an account.'

I went to the registration page and started the teaching journey.

'What do you want for your login name?' I asked.

'Chris Steward.'

I rolled my eyes; I had a feeling that I was teaching a cat to use the computer.

'You don't use your real name as your login name. Can you think of something other than your name?'

'Anna Bell.'

'Other than my name, please.' I wanted to slam the MacBook in his face.

'Snowball.'

I nodded and quickly typed in 'Snowball'.

I said, 'Snowball has been taken, let's use "snowball1234".'

He nodded.

'What do you want for the password?'

'Snowball1234.'

'You know hackers love people like you.' I rolled my eyes. 'You can't use your login name for the password.'

'This is so troublesome!' Chris leaned back on the sofa like a deflated balloon.

'Come on, just make up some word combination,' I said to calm him.

He thought for a while and turned to me.

'When is your birthday?'

'Twelfth of July, why?'

'Put "Silly1207" for my password.' He grinned. 'This is actually a great one – I think I'll change all my passwords to that.'

He took out his phone and started changing the password on his email account.

I glared at him but was unable to stop the smile on my face.

The thought of Chris using my birthday as his password felt a bit strange and ... slightly thrilling.

After we completed the registration, we went to the next step – shopping.

'So you choose what you want and add it to the shopping cart.' I demonstrated the procedure to Chris.

Surprisingly, he was paying full attention to my tutorial.

'If you want to buy more than one item, you can add the number here.'

'Oh, I see.'

While Chris had his focus on the computer screen, I took a peek at him. That was when I realised how close we were sitting.

He was leaning towards me; one of his arms was on the table, and the other was on the back of my chair, just as if he was wrapping me in his arm.

'May I try?'

Before I could react, Chris moved even closer. His head was just above my shoulder, and his chest touched my back. The scent of his cologne was so strong, it made me realise this was the closest physical contact I'd had with him.

Forget about all that heart-pounding; my body had literally frozen.

I wasn't scared of men and hadn't had any bad experiences; in fact, I was quite good at dealing with them. The only person that made me act weird was him, Chris Steward. Simply his appearance would mess up my mind.

'This was the part where I got stuck,' he groaned.

'After you input the credit card number, you'll need to unlock your phone to approve the payment on the app.'

I looked at the payment page and showed him the instructions.

Chris nodded and unlocked his phone.

I took the mouse and started typing the credit card number.

'It should be five over there.' Chris placed his hand on mine and moved the mouse to highlight the incorrect number. After that, he looked at his phone and waited for the approval request.

I kept visibly calm, but underneath my peaceful face, my mind repeatedly screamed:

Chris Steward touched my hand

Chris Steward touched my hand

Chris Steward touched my hand!

My heart beat like a galloping horse and my blood pressure spiked faster than a rocket. Before today, it never occurred to me that Chris could have such a deep effect on me, and my fear of overly caring for him became a warning alert.

'Approved.' Chris was ecstatic.

'Great.' I smiled, trying to act normal.

'Since you have helped me, I will return you a favour as a thank-you,' he said.

'It's fine, no need.' I laughed while packing away my laptop.

'Oh, come on.'

I softly shook my head and walked to the kitchen. As I turned around, my face almost slammed into his chest.

'Oh, my!' I screamed and my hand landed on his chest. 'What the hell you are doing behind me?'

'Well, I was waiting to hear your wish.' He didn't move an inch and stapled his gaze on me.

Since we were standing so close to each other, I had to tilt my head to see his face.

'No, really it's fine.' I gently pushed his chest, hoping he could leave my personal space, but he stood rock still.

The next second was like a scene in a romantic movie; he grabbed my wrist and gently pulled my hand up to his lips. Before I could react, he dropped a kiss on the back of my hand.

The intimacy of this immediately overtook my brain, and I was no longer able to think properly.

Did he just kiss my hand? I repeatedly asked myself.

'Do you want more?' An evil smile appeared as his lips left my flesh.

'Wh … what?' I wanted to beat myself for that shaky voice.

He didn't answer my question. Instead, he pulled me to

him and wrapped his arms around my waist – we were close enough to feel each other's heartbeat.

'Do you want more?' he repeated, and this time, he cupped my face and slid his finger across my lips. 'Here?' He smiled.

The air felt thin and my dizziness had returned. If he had not held my waist, I would probably have fallen to the floor.

Our gaze had been locked for too long and I felt heat in my body. Slowly, he lowered his head and landed his lips on my cheek.

'You are a silly girl,' he whispered in my ear and released me.

I came to as he left my personal space and my thinking ability bounced back.

You are a silly girl.

I analysed his words, but they just confused me.

'What do you mean?' I frowned.

'You just let a grown man into your house and get so close to you?' Chris said in a stern voice.

I shot him a confused look.

'What I meant was, you shouldn't just let some guy in your house and let them get so close to you. You should keep some distance.'

The authoritative tone sounded like a father or brother teaching me personal safety.

'Well, it's fine, I know how to protect myself.' I chuckled.

'It doesn't seem like it to me, though. You let me get so close to you.' He furrowed his brow. 'If it was a creepy man, you would be in danger.'

Is he worried about me? Why?

Hundreds of reasons flipped through my head and I smiled at the one that made me flush.

It had been a while since I had been taken care of. I thought I didn't mind being on my own until today, when he used just a few words to demolish the walls that I'd built up for years. I was moved by his words. Even with the danger warning in my head that his feelings might vanish after tonight, I wanted to be true to him for once.

I steadied my gaze on him, ignoring all the fear that quietly grew inside me. 'I let you in because I trusted you.'

The devil widened his eyes for a second, but slowly, an evil smile took over and it once again sped up my heart rate.

***

'Make a wish, Anna,' my mum whispered into my ear.

I woke up in the middle of the night, cold sweat sliding down my forehead, I let out a deep breath and glanced at the calendar on the wall.

Twelfth of July.

It was that time again. The worst day of my life.

Each year at this time, I would bury myself in work – with no celebration, wishes or presents. This was the best way to get through the day.

This year, nothing had changed. My schedule was packed with jobs; one thing great about working for Chris was there was no resting time. The tiring schedule was the best birthday gift this year.

I dragged myself out of bed and put on my usual all-black clothing. Every movement I made was slow and forced, and my limbs felt heavier than usual. 'It will be a long day,' I said to myself as I walked out of my flat.

When I got to the studio, Chris was already there. He smiled broadly at me, perhaps a little too enthusiastically.

'What?' I asked and checked myself in the mirror.

'Nothing.' Chris smiled. 'I am just hungry.'

'Take this.' I threw him my sandwich, but he threw it back to me. 'Fine, just starve yourself then.'

'Hey, I saw a great restaurant on Facebook. Want to check it out tonight?' Chris suggested while playing with his phone.

'Um...' My mood dropped immediately. I didn't want to go anywhere nice. I just wanted to sleep through the day. 'Maybe some other day,' I replied.

'Why?' Chris frowned.

Usually, I would think of some ridiculous reason, but not today. 'I'm meeting someone tonight.' If I made an excuse, hopefully, he would leave me alone.

'Who?' Chris asked as if he were a concerned parent.

'A friend,' I lied.

'Which friend?'

'A friend!' I groaned like a rebellious teenager.

Chris stared at me angrily. I was confused about where his rage came from.

'I thought you didn't have a boyfriend?' he asked in a stern voice.

'Huh? No, I don't have a boyfriend.' I squinted. 'Where did that come from?'

Chris breathed out a long breath and relaxed his brow, but was still looking strict. 'Then who are you meeting today?'

'What's the matter with you today?' I gasped.

Chris stared at me, pouting his lips and clenching his jaw. Seconds passed, and I crossed my arms waiting for his answer. He eventually cracked. 'I just want to celebrate your birthday with you.'

I gawked at him, not knowing what to say.

'Who are you meeting tonight?' Chris fired the question like a machine gun, the anger in his eyes making him look as if he wanted to eat me alive.

'A friend,' I repeated.

'Which friend?'

I groaned at our ridiculous and time-wasting conversation. 'No one. I just made it up. I'm not meeting anyone. Okay? Are you satisfied?' I put my hand over my forehead to cool it down.

Chris had gone quiet, but not for long. 'Am I boring you?'

'What?' I looked at him, confused. 'No, just...' I wanted to swallow what I was about to say, but the words rushed out before I could stop them. 'I don't celebrate my birthday. My parents died on my birthday twenty years ago.'

The surroundings became silent and the air clotted.

Chris's beautiful eyes were wide as coins. He was completely nonplussed by my answer. 'Sorry, I...' The sorrow on his face showed his regret for once again touching my scar.

The guilt on his face softened me. 'It's fine, just forget about it.'

He didn't say another word throughout that day.

After we finished all our jobs, Chris offered to drive me home.

'Anna...' He broke the silence but weirdly. 'Um...'

'What?'

Chris was mumbling and this was not like him. 'I know you don't want to celebrate your birthday today, but would you be okay to celebrate Snowball's birthday?'

'Sure,' I answered, feeling awkward. 'When is that?'

'Today,' he said.

I looked at him, confused.

'My vet reminded me yesterday.'

The embarrassed look on his face proved that it was a lie. He must have made it up just now.

What a tacky excuse.

'I'm sure he did.' I laughed.

'It is.' Chris smiled with embarrassment, and a faint reddish shimmer rose across his cheeks.

I couldn't stop laughing. He soon followed, and we both cried with laughter.

His persistence in wanting to celebrate my birthday was adorable. The lie was ridiculous yet sweet.

'Thank you,' I said.

Chris nodded awkwardly. 'Are you okay to celebrate Snowball's birthday at my house?'

I smiled. 'Sure.'

On the way to his, we stopped by a Chinese restaurant and ordered takeaway.

When we arrived at his house, Snowball ran up and gave me a warm welcome again, at the same time trying to get his mouth on the takeaway we'd ordered.

'I am sorry, sweetie, this is not for you.' I stroked his fur to calm him.

He woofed.

'Okay, maybe a little bit. Come on.' Chris laughed.

I settled on the couch and Snowball jumped up to sit next to me.

'Fine, I'll take the other side.' Chris sat next to me.

After we finished our food, Chris passed me a glass of wine and led me to the balcony.

The beautiful city was under our feet, light from the buildings and houses scattered like Christmas lights. I looked up to the cloudless sky decorated with sparkling stars, and memories of my parents rose faintly.

It was a summer night. We lay in a field, cherishing the blanket of stars.

'Make a wish, Anna,' my mum whispered in my ear.

It was a birthday trip, and also our last ever trip together.

I took a sip of the wine and swallowed down the liquid and my tears. A memory that I had almost forgotten had made its way to my head.

'Thank you.' I kept my gaze on the buildings and trapped my tears in my eyes.

'Anna.' The tenderness in Chris's voice softened my guard. An urge to cry rose from my senses. 'I am sorry for your loss,' he said.

The feeling of sadness overwhelmed my body and the tears finally dropped like rainfall.

I guessed my sudden emotional breakdown had scared Chris. He stood like a statue for a minute, and after he regained himself, he came towards me and wrapped me in his arms. He stroked my back; it was comforting and slowed the fall of my tears.

'I am useless.' I gave him a sheepish grin.

'No. You are not.' He tightened his arms around me. 'If your parents were still here, they would be proud.'

I laughed, shaking my head.

'I mean it,' he said. 'You are clever, hardworking...' He paused when his fingers slid across my cheek. 'And beautiful.'

The intimate gesture immediately turned me into a fireball and heat flowed through my body.

'Chris...' I searched his face, trying to find hints of deception. But then, my eyes landed on his lips, and weirdly, I wondered whether his lips tasted like honeycomb. The sudden thirst for honey threatened to turn me into a bear. I bit my lip, trying to suppress my urge to taste those sweet lips.

Chris's face came closer to mine, and in a flash, his lips touched mine.

He kissed me.

CHAPTER FIVE

'So...' A beautiful blonde stepped closer to Chris. Her ocean-blue eyes sparkled under long lashes, blinking as if in invitation to him. 'I am alone tonight. Would you like to come over to my place?' She laid her hand on his bare chest and slid her red-nail-polished finger across his sculpted torso like a seductive snake.

Chris abruptly grabbed her hand and pushed her away. 'Miss, I think you have misunderstood.' He patted his chest like patting off dust. 'You are not her.' He turned and was about to leave to room.

'Who is she?' she shouted in rage; no words could describe her anger.

Chris turned his head and gave her an evil grin. 'You will see.'

'*Cut!*' a man with a space-ball cap shouted. 'Five minutes break, everyone.' He was the director of the movie.

The ambient sound was raised. Everyone relaxed and some started to prepare for the next scene.

I walked over to Chris and took care of his make-up.

'Do you know it's Alex Smith's birthday this Friday?' the beautiful blonde asked Chris.

She was supposed to be in the changing room, but instead, she had stuck around near Chris.

'Yes. I know he's having a party—'

'You're invited too?' She seemed thrilled.

Chris tightened his lips; I knew by this look that he didn't like her interruption.

'Yes, I was in—'

She interrupted again. 'Would you like to go together? I'm invited too.' She looked up at him with sparkling puppy eyes.

It was obvious that she was into him, and for sure Chris knew it.

He steadied his gaze on the blonde and melted her heart before he even spoke. 'Do you ever let men finish –' he looked at her with an evil grin '– a sentence?'

I had my back to the blonde, but I would have bet anything her face flushed bright red.

'I'm sorry. I have a date already.' Chris smiled as he politely rejected the girl.

'It's fine.' Blondie's tone was full of disappointment.

Blondie's assistant finally came over to pull her away. 'Hey, you should be in the changing room.'

About time!

'What are you doing this Friday?' Chris said after looking left and right, making sure no one was near us.

'Stuff,' I said in a cold voice.

I didn't know why my tummy felt sick when I saw the blonde flirting with him. He had not made the first move. Besides, he rejected her right in front of me, obviously to reassure me about our relationship. I should be contented.

But my insecure personality wouldn't stop thinking of him being chased after by thousands of women.

Chris studied my face and chuckled. 'Jealous?'

'Of who?' I sneered at him.

He gazed at me with an evil smile. 'Do you need me to take you right here to prove myself to you?'

His words were like a drumstick, pounding my heart. But I didn't want him to know I had just surrendered to his charms and the fact that I would cheer if he did as he said.

'Chris,' the director shouted from ten feet away. He pointed one finger in the air, gesturing for us to be ready in one minute.

'What a shame,' I whispered into his ear, not worrying what he would do or say about my teasing because he was about to dive back into his work. 'It would be fun if you did.'

He looked at me and slowly gave me a small, flirty smirk. 'You are in so much trouble.'

I didn't know how long we had been kissing, but our lips hadn't been apart for so long that mine felt numb.

'So you wanted me to do this at the shoot today? Huh?' Chris mumbled as he buried his head in my neck. The tickling feeling from his breath made me moan.

'No...' My trembling voice sounded powerless.

He chuckled and then landed his lips on mine again. He kissed me until Snowball couldn't take the jealousy and stuck his head in between us.

'Okay,' Chris said as Snowball licked my face. 'You know

you can't compete with me.' He tried to pull Snowball away from me. 'Go away, otherwise no treat.'

Snowball woofed when Chris pulled him.

He chuckled. 'Fine. You first then.'

I embraced my white furry friend in my arms and popped a kiss on his forehead.

Chris watched in silence. His stare was naked and steamy; the power of his eyes could speed up my heartbeat without trying.

'What?' I looked away to stop the heat building up on my face.

'Do you want to go public?'

His questions left me gaping in surprise because this wasn't what we usually talked about.

'Go public about us?' I needed to reassure myself what he was referring to, though I thought I already had the answer.

'No, about you dating Snowball.' Chris rolled his eyes. 'Of course about us, you silly girl.'

I punched him with my forceless fist and hid my true feelings with a scoff.

Not that I wanted to hide our relationship, on the contrary, I would have loved to tell every woman to stay away from him. But even if he announced it to the world, I doubted any woman would take me seriously and keep their distance. For the worst, they might even take their chance because they saw no threat. So what was the point? I might even become the target of his fans, or even lose my job.

'So?' he asked.

'No thank you.' I held my palm up to him.

But perhaps I should have sugar-coated my words; his face dropped.

'Being with me must be hard for you,' he said in a cold voice.

I took a deep breath, debating in my head whether to tell him the truth or not. I probably took too long because he leaned back with crossed arms.

'You need to think?' He squinted.

'Yes.'

'Yes? You feel it's difficult being with me?' He raised his voice and his eyebrows.

'No.' I took a breath. 'I mean, yes, I need to think about the answer, but not because I think it's hard being your girlfriend. I just think it's too early to go public – we haven't been together long. I think we should take it slow.'

Chris looked at me full of disappointment, but he smiled and nodded. 'Okay, but can I tell my parents and siblings?'

Though I thought it was still too early to tell, I agreed because I didn't want to further disappoint him.

★ ★ ★ ★

The thirtieth of October was a big day.

But not for me. It was a big day for Chris.

'It's not a big day, it's just my birthday.' He laughed while driving us to work.

'It's *the* Chris Steward's birthday.' I widened my eyes.

'Fine, what do you want?' he asked.

'I want to celebrate with you,' I said. 'But I know you have a tight schedule so just tell me which day you're available.'

'What?' Chris frowned. 'You're my girlfriend – of course I'm celebrating with you on my actual birthday.'

'Well...' I tried not to sound jealous. 'You are a busy man with lots of fans.'

I had been dating Chris for a couple of months, and with all the love he gave me, I knew he was serious about our relationship. But his job involved countless attractive women, and witnessing all the flirtation between them burned me to ash. Those women kept coming, and even though Chris made zero response, they never gave up and grabbed any chance to flirt with him. The jealousy was unnecessary and my worries were delusional, yet it was still painful to watch.

Perhaps my bitterness had shown on my face. Chris glanced at me and burst into laughter as he pulled over into a car park.

'Yes, Ms Bell, I have lots of fans and girlfriends – they're lining up to celebrate with me.' He flashed his signature evil grin again, seducing my inner desire and speeding up my heart rate. His fond gaze steadied on me, those olive eyes sparkling with playful amusement. I hated it when he teased me, yet I still had a strong affection for that attractive face. Simply a smile from him would erase all my jealousy.

I clicked my tongue to divert my true feelings; I never liked to show my vulnerable side.

'Come on, you know I don't mean that,' I said.

I put on a stern expression, but his seductive face heated my face again.

'Then what do you mean?' he asked. He lifted my hand and planted a kiss on the back of it. 'Let me guess, are you trying to ask whether I would date a fan or a co-star? The answer is no.' He smiled. 'One silly girl is enough – I don't have time for another.' He poked my nose and laughed.

In the end, we decided to celebrate his birthday at his flat and I would stay overnight. It would be my first night at his place. The thought of sleeping next to him made my heart pound.

His birthday fell on a Sunday, which gave me sufficient time to pack my sleepover items. We would be ordering food, so I didn't need to worry about cooking. But I didn't want to go empty-handed. I therefore baked him a cake and bought a present. But I wondered if he would like my gift since he was wealthy enough to own everything.

On the day of his birthday, I arrived a little early at his apartment. I nervously pulled my miniskirt and straightened my hair with my palm. When Chris opened the door, Snowball rushed out to welcome me. His smile and wagging tail quickly demolished my anxiety.

'Hey, baby.' I petted his head while he leaned towards the cake and took a few sniffs.

'I don't think that's for you, boy,' Chris teased.

He wore a soft white jumper and a pair of blue jeans. His skin was soft and smooth, stunning even without make-up.

'Let me take it.' Chris took the cake and led me into his flat.

The place was in darkness, and soft blues music was playing in the background. Dim light was coming from the dining room. We followed the light and when I saw the room set-up, I gasped.

The dining table was perfectly set with burning white candles; cutlery was neatly arranged like in a fine-dining restaurant; a big bouquet of red roses lay on one side of the table, fluttering with the scent of flowery sweetness. I took a breath to enjoy this romantic heaven; it was then I realised our dinner was ready in the open kitchen. Steam was curling up from inch-thick steaks; chips were fried beautifully golden and were placed neatly on an elegant white plate waiting to be served.

'Chris?' My voice went up. 'I thought we were ordering food?'

Chris shot me a sheepish smile. 'I changed my mind. I wanted to cook for you.'

'On your birthday?'

'Yes.' He pulled out a chair for me. 'Seeing you happy is the best gift for me.'

His words sped up my heart, yet I simply smiled to hide the madness in my mind.

As soon as I sat down, he gave me the bouquet. I embraced the sweet scent of roses and admired the smoothness of the red velvet petals; though it was not my favourite flower, joy filled my heart.

It was the first time I had been given flowers. I brought the bouquet close to enjoy the touch of nature and I counted the number of blooms. I was surprised to discover that there were fifty stems.

'It must have been very expensive,' I said. 'It's your birthday, why did you buy roses for me?'

'Who said they're for you? I bought them for myself.' He smirked. 'I'm just lending them to you to take a look.'

I giggled. 'Okay, I'll return your roses.' I placed them next to him.

He walked over to me with a smile, leaned down and planted a kiss on my lips.

'They're for you, you silly girl.'

The small gesture made my heart pound again.

I started to worry I would have a heart problem very soon if it kept pounding as though I was having a heart attack.

The dinner was amazing and it seemed that cooking was another of Chris's talents. I became nervous when I saw him take his last bite of steak.

'I saw you brought dessert.' Chris smiled.

'Yep. Let me get it.' I went to the kitchen and brought out a five-inch-high cake covered with white cream and strawberries. Written in icing was 'Happy Birthday Chris'.

I lit the candle and sang 'Happy Birthday' as I approached him with the cake.

He turned his head in surprise and quickly flashed me a smile when he saw the cake.

'Make a wish before blowing,' I reminded him.

At first, he was reluctant and wanted to just eat the cake. But with my bravado and nerve staring him down, in the end, he had no choice but to make his wish and blow out the candle.

When he could finally put the strawberry sponge cake into his mouth, he chuckled. 'Why did you insist on me making a wish?' he asked.

A long-gone memory flashed in my mind, and a familiar voice whispered in my ear.

Make a wish, Anna.

'You don't want to waste a once-a-year chance to make a wish.' I forced a smile.

Chris looked at me in silence and didn't ask any further questions.

Before we finished the cake, I passed him a small box wrapped in blue paper.

'You've bought me a gift?' he said with a big smile and a sparkle in his eyes. His animated and exaggerated acting had me wondering if he already knew I'd bought him a birthday gift.

'You knew?' I asked.

All his focus was on the box; he didn't seem to have heard my question. The only sound was the rustle of paper as he tore away the gift wrap. He took out a green jewellery box. 'If this is a ring, you'll need to propose before I say yes.' He laughed.

When he took out a necklace from the box, he tilted his head quizzically.

'Is this pendant a four-leaf clover?' He took it in his hand and studied it carefully as if it was a fossil.

'Yep.' I nodded with a smile.

'Why?'

'Well...' I considered my answer cautiously because I didn't want to risk any tears today. 'A four-leaf clover is a rare plant and that's why it represents good luck.'

'I don't need luck.' Chris grinned.

'You don't need luck,' I said. 'You just need to be safe.'

Chris looked at the necklace and seemed engrossed in his thoughts. As I was thinking of explaining my point without sounding too depressing, he slowly looked up and locked eyes with me.

All misunderstandings seemed silently gone.

'Can you help me?' Chris asked.

I took the necklace and clasped it around his neck. When I was done, Chris grabbed my hand and pulled it to his lips.

'Thank you.' He dropped a kiss on my hand.

I pulled him up from the chair and wrapped my arms around his neck, hugging him close to me, chest to chest. 'No, thank you,' I whispered.

'Why?' he asked, sliding his arm to my waist.

I looked at this beautiful man, grateful that my life had taken a U-turn after meeting him. In all the years of living in my sorrowful past, it never occurred to me that I would one day fall in love like others. I could not foresee the future; no one knew if Chris and I could be happy ever after, yet even if our relationship was just for a second or a moment, the happiness I had right now ensured I would not regret meeting him.

I tiptoed and slowly planted a kiss on him.

'Thank you for being in my life.'

Things were pretty good between me and Chris. After seeing each other for about six months, he asked me to move into his house. My instinct told me it might be too early for that, yet knowing I could take care of Snowball, I agreed. Living with Chris was full of joy; this was the first time in my life I felt I was being taken care of.

Even though his demanding boss attitude made my work life hell, any time after that he was the best caring boyfriend. He would cook a healthy dinner, comfort me when I was sad, answer any questions I had, and also give me personal space.

But happiness never lasts.

The day started as any normal morning but ended in rage.

'Anna!'

A handsome man in his mid-forties was waving at me. His shoulder-length wavy dark brown hair was in a casual style, his jawbone was strong and edgy and his thin lips formed a grin. I returned a smile, which triggered his dark brown eyes to glow with excitement.

'Derek!' I hugged him as I spoke. He slid his arm around my waist and it stayed there after our hug.

'You're working here today?' he asked.

'Yes.' I leaned back subtly, hoping he would notice my hint to withdraw his arm, but he didn't. I had known Derek for quite a while, so for sure he was not taking advantage of me, and from what I'd heard, he was truly a model gentleman. But today, his passion made me worry what others might think, and the other I was thinking of was...

Chris's voice came from behind me. 'Where have you been?'

Derek and I looked at the source of the voice.

Chris stared at me with the sternest face I had ever seen. The tenderness in his olive eyes had vanished, and they were instead filled with anger.

My natural reaction was to apologise. 'Sorry, I—'

'Sorry, it was my fault,' Derek said. 'Let me introduce myself—'

'Derek Slone,' Chris said. 'The director of *Rosie*, I know. Chris Steward. Nice to meet you.'

Chris took a glance at me while shaking hands with Derek. The tension in his jawline shouted his negative feelings toward this guy.

'We never get a chance to meet, Mr Steward.' Derek pulled up a businesslike face.

'Call me Chris.' Chris was not much different; their professional attitude grew apparent; they were both naturals in a formal situation. 'Though we've never met before, I see fate has pulled us together today,' Chris said.

Derek smiled at me, his eyes sparkling like black diamonds. 'Yes, she is my angel.' Derek gave me a wink.

'Stop messing with me, Derek.' I laughed and pinched him on his arm.

He grabbed my hand and held it in his palm.

'Um, I'm sorry for interrupting you guys but I think our director wants to start soon, so we better get going.' Chris looked at me sternly, telling me there would be lots of explanations later. 'Nice to meet you, Derek.' He grabbed my arm, forcing me to follow him as he spoke.

'Sure.' I nodded to Chris and half ran to keep up with him.

'I'm sorry, Derek, another day.' I waved goodbye to Derek and tried to give him the politest response I could.

'No worries, sweetheart.' Derek smirked. 'I'll call you later.'

An evil grin slowly rose on Derek's face; the flirty look on him made my eyes widen and my brows flew up to my hairline.

Sweetheart? Did I hear that right?

Chris pulled me into his changing room and slammed the door behind me. When he let go of my hand, the hard grip had left a sore red mark. I tried to ease the pain by massaging it with the other hand. His aggressive reaction made me wonder whether it was my lateness to work that had made him jumpy or if Derek's excessive friendliness had set him off. Standing behind him made it impossible for me to detect the truth.

'*Sweetheart?*' He turned around, and the fire in his eyes could have burned me to death. 'Did you fail to mention you're dating someone else?' His eyes were charged with rage. His lips tightened up after each word, and I could even see blood flooding the vein on his forehead.

Okay, he was mad about Derek.

'Derek is just a friend,' I said. 'Oh, he was the friend who gave me the whisky.'

Have you ever tried to put out a fire by pouring water on it, but accidentally poured vodka instead? Well, I guessed I just did the latter.

'He was the one who gave you the seven-hundred-pound whisky?' Chris thundered. He was beyond angry and his hair looked as if it was on fire. 'And you're telling me you two are just friends? Are you sure he wasn't expecting something else?' he shouted – well, it was more like screaming. He was so loud that I worried the people in the room next door might hear us. Changing rooms usually had thin walls with no soundproofing.

I held up a finger to my lips, trying to lower his volume. 'Calm down.'

'What, are you scared your *friend* will hear us? Is that why you don't want to go public? You worry he will know?'

'What?' I rolled my eyes. 'He's just a friend I met at work. Besides, he just hired me for a birthday party, nothing else. I haven't seen him since I started working with you.'

'He never calls you?' he shouted at me, looking sceptical.

The fact was, he did, though he just called to talk about freelance jobs, but my instinct told me this might not be the best time to be an honest child. We had added enough vodka to the fire.

'No.' I looked down to the floor, playing with my fingers. I'm a terrible liar.

'You should work on your acting skills,' he said sternly. 'Or maybe you could ask him to teach you!'

'Chris...'

'I can't talk to you right now.' He dashed out of the room as he spoke and left me in there feeling useless and alone.

However, that was not the end of the day. There were still a couple of scenes before we could call it a day.

Even though I knew Chris was enraged, he didn't show it on his face, not even slightly. When the crew was around, he even talked to me as usual, but strictly work-related, obviously. He was an extraordinary actor on stage, but never occurred to me that he could be magnificent off stage as well.

After he finished his last scene, I went into his changing room to grab my stuff. Then I realised he had left without saying goodbye.

CHAPTER SIX

Did your wise parents tell you not to move in with a guy before you had built a strong relationship? I had lost both of mine at a young age, so there wasn't anyone to teach me this.

After Chris had stormed out, I had no chance to talk with him about our issue. If I hadn't been living with him, I could just have let him cool down and waited until the next day to show up with my apology face.

But I needed to face him tonight. The thought of being confronted by him frightened me. I worried about what we would get into, how bad the situation would be and whether he would dump me. If so, I would need to find a place to move into because I had already given up my apartment.

A notification came from my phone and a message popped up on my screen. It was from Chris.

> I am staying at a hotel tonight, please feed Snowball. Thanks.

Reading this message should have relieved my worries,

but instead, I was disappointed. The feeling of abandonment was growing at a steady speed.

I let out a deep breath, facing the fact that I would be alone tonight. Well, not completely alone. I still had Snowball.

After doing all the housework, mopping the floor, having a shower and tucking in Snowball, my long-gone feeling of loneliness slowly returned. I lay on the king-size bed and looked blankly at the ceiling. The mild scent of Chris's shampoo rose from the pillow next to me. I rolled to my side and buried my head in his pillow, breathing in the remaining scent and remembering happy moments with him.

Snowball jumped onto the bed and emitted a soft woof; he lay next to me and put his head on my pillow.

'Fine, you take mine and I'll take his.' I looked into his big black eyes and couldn't stop wondering what his roommate was doing right now. I grabbed the phone from the bedside drawer and thought about what to text him.

Maybe I can explain myself? But then that would be a long text. How about just an apology? But it seems rude to do it over a text?

After a long debate in my head, I finally dared to type in one word.

> Goodnight.

I thought he would be generous enough to reply to my text. But I might have underestimated his temper. I fell asleep with an empty mailbox.

The next morning, I was awakened by the licking alarm.

'Good morning, Snowball.' I gently patted his head. But

he shook my hand away, telling me that he was not asking for a pat. 'Breakfast, I know.'

But before feeding him, I decided to do something more important.

I grabbed my phone that was next to the bed. As soon as I saw a message on the screen, my heart raced, but it died down quickly as I realised it was a sale notification from a shopping app.

I opened the texting app and saw the double blue ticks next to my last message, meaning Chris had seen the message but decided not to text back.

He probably saw the goodnight text this morning, so it would be weird to reply, I convinced myself, trying to believe this was what happened, otherwise, my insecurity would eat me alive.

After Snowball was fed, it was time to get dressed. I sat in front of the mirror and sighed at my dry skin, dark eye bags and wrinkles; every part of my face screamed sleepiness. If I wanted to win back his heart, this face would need a magic makeover.

I lifted my magic wand and started by smoothing my skin with foundation, brightening my eyes with concealer, drawing cat-eyes eyeliner, and lastly brushing a pink shimmer on my cheek as a final touch.

I didn't want to lose Chris, not because of some random friend. But my low self-esteem needed this makeover to build my courage to get close to him.

How pathetic!

No driver meant public transport. I decided to take the Tube today.

The temperature in the Tube in spring should have been

cool, but the busy crowd in the morning made it impossible to breathe.

I stood at the side near the exit door, trying to grab as much air as possible whenever the door opened.

There were still a couple of stops before mine, so I took the spare time to think about the conversation we could have today.

Would he consider dumping me after a night of thinking? Or would he forgive me? Should I start looking for an apartment?

If he dumped me, could I still work with him? Maybe I should take a day off to cry while looking for an apartment.

I wonder what the real estate agent would think if her customer complimented the property with tears in her eyes.

My silly imagination surprisingly made me smile. I couldn't believe I still had the capacity to make jokes about myself when I might become homeless very soon.

I looked up to check the station, and a cute-looking man standing opposite flashed me a smile. *Do I have dirt on my face or does my stupid face make him laugh?*

As we arrived at my stop, I jumped off the Tube without making further eye contact. I was lucky that the shooting location was in central London and could be reached that way. Otherwise, I would have needed to take an Uber, and my company wouldn't cover the fee.

When I arrived at work, I was surprised to see that I was one of the earliest staff to arrive, even though I took public transport. Taking my time, I leisurely took out my case and laid out all my equipment, so I could start right away when Chris appeared. Just as I was almost done, I heard a familiar voice.

'You left early today?'

I turned around and saw Chris in a black T-shirt and

jeans. He probably bought them yesterday so he wouldn't need to return home.

'Yes.' *Did he come by the house this morning to pick me up? Or maybe he just came to check on Snowball.*

'You went home this morning?' I asked, hoping he would give the answer I wished for.

But he shared no response, only stared at my face in silence.

'Going somewhere today?' he asked abruptly.

'No.'

I tightened my lips to withhold a smile from appearing on my face.

My effort seemed to be working; at least he noticed me.

For the next thirty minutes, there was silence, and I took this chance to put my small joy on hold and focus all my attention on my work.

Work before love. I didn't want to discuss our feelings at work – I hated to cry in front of a bunch of co-workers, and Chris hated to mix personal feelings with work.

After I was done, he went out to the shoot. I stood behind the crew but glued my eyes on Chris in case there were any modifications needed.

As soon as the shooting started, my anxiety relaxed. His serious attitude was too intimidating and made me nervous.

Chris was posing for the front cover of the magazine; the glow and shine on him was the best scenery. The assistants who stood next to me gossiped about his love life, guessing if he was dating a supermodel.

No one would ever imagine he was dating me. A small potato that no one had heard of, not to mention my ordinary outlook and cardboard cut-out figure. Seriously, Chris might have some issues with his taste in women.

Once the photographer paused the shoot, all the supporting crew rushed to the centre to adjust the setting for the next shoot. I followed them and took my set of cosmetics to Chris.

'Dinner tonight?' Chris asked after the lighting man was out of earshot.

I paused and nodded.

After I was done, the next round of shooting started.

Did he make up his mind and decide to dump me? But he could just dump me instead of treating me to dinner.

Who said anything about treating me, maybe we'll split the bill?

My mind raced like a flashlight on a camera. I wanted to go home and sleep through all the issues but more interviews were waiting for us. Shortly after the shoot finished, we headed for the second interview at a radio station, and there was more after until 6.30 p.m.

'I'll wait for you in the car,' Chris said while I was packing my work case.

After he left the room, I fell onto a seat like a deflated balloon. Today's packed schedule had kept me busy from thinking about dinner tonight. I had almost forgotten about it.

What should I say to him?

The thought of our speechless stares once again put me under pressure.

A mobile buzz pulled me back from my thoughts. It was a message from Chris.

Are you ready?

I quickly stuffed everything into the case and rushed to his car.

'Sorry, I lost one of my brushes.' I tried to cover up for my late show-up.

But Chris didn't say a word. He waited for me to sort the seat belt and drove us to the restaurant.

We arrived at the pub where we went for our first dinner. His friend Richard warmly welcomed us as usual.

'I see you brought your little friend again.' Richard smiled.

'Not a friend,' Chris glanced at me. 'She's my girlfriend.'

Richard and I both widened our eyes and raised our eyebrows. One might expect that Richard would be surprised, but it must have looked weird that I had a shocked face too.

Richard looked at me and chuckled. 'Did you know about this? Or did he make it up?'

I realised my expression might have been too dramatic, but no words could describe my surprise. I said nothing but flashed him a sheepish smile.

'Stop messing around and feed us.' Chris grinned.

After we were seated, Chris ordered a burger for each of us. Then we fell into the silent game again.

I wasn't very hungry, but I wished the food would come sooner so that I wouldn't need to sit here and stare at my fingers.

My mind wandered off, guessing what he might say. He would probably say he was disappointed in me or that I was a bad girlfriend *blah blah blah*.

Chris interrupted my dark thoughts. 'So you and Derek ... how did you guys meet?'

Transparent, straight to the point, not hiding his curiosity.

I owed him a truthful answer.

'We met a couple of years ago when I was working freelance for an advertising firm. He was the director of the TVC and I was their make-up artist.' I let out a breath, trying to calm my nerves before I continued. 'After the shooting, we talked for hours. I can't remember what I said, but he seemed amazed by my experience and asked me to work with him on his next movie.'

'Which one?'

'*The Outsider*,' I said. 'But everything we talked about or planned was purely work, I promise.'

'But you two looked so much closer than just colleagues.' Chris spilled his doubt. 'You can't fool me.' He smirked.

I shook my head quickly. 'I'm not lying. Nothing happened between us,' I continued. 'But we worked a few more times after that movie. And last year he asked me for a favour to help his sister plan a kids' party.'

Chris stared at his glass of water thoughtfully. His silence once again gave me a headache. I looked to the kitchen, praying for the arrival of my food.

'Did he contact you when you worked with me?'

Here we go.

No matter how unwilling I was, the truth would need to come out today.

'Yes.' I looked down at my fingers. 'He called to see if I could help him with some freelance job. But I wasn't available because we were busy shooting *Cruel Mind*.' I peeked at Chris to check his reaction to my answer.

Chris once again sank into his thoughts.

Was this how it would be for tonight? He asked questions, I answered then we went silent, repeated multiple times. It felt like an interrogation.

'That's it?' he said. 'He never called you again?'

I gulped. He was getting close.

'Well...' I hesitated, not willing to pour vodka on fire again. 'He did.'

'And?' I think Chris knew he was getting to the answer; he leaned forward without obviously putting pressure on me.

'He invited me to dinner.'

'Alone?'

I nodded.

'That's a date! And you're still telling me there's nothing between you two?' He lowered his voice but the anger lingered in his words.

'Yes, because I turned him down. And he just laughed about it. Maybe he was just making fun of me anyway. There is nothing between us.' I sighed. 'Chris, I'm sorry I didn't tell you yesterday because I knew how it might sound, and I didn't want you to get the wrong idea.'

He looked at me; the olive eyes were soft with tenderness, but his face was still serious as hell. 'You know I hate it that you hid things from me.' He relaxed more as he spoke. 'But did he still call you?'

I shook my head. 'No, yesterday was the first time I talked to him after that call.'

Chris took a deep breath, then he looked at the waitress and nodded his head.

'Anna.' He looked into my eyes and gently placed his palm on mine. 'Don't ever lie to me again.'

Food was served right after he spoke. It looked delicious, but my appetite vanished because of his undertone of warning.

Everything returned to normal after our conversation, or at least it seemed to.

Our relationship returned to how it was before, but once a bad seed was planted in the love bed, it would eventually move its way up to the light.

The Derek incident made me nervous about bumping into him again, especially when Chris was around. Not that I had any feelings for Derek, but the fact that Chris pointed out he might have feelings for me had me worried.

I never imagined anyone would like me, not a celebrity, director or any human. My low self-esteem had grown inside me ever since my parents' accident, and the thought of never being loved was imprinted in my head. This was also a reason I joined the make-up industry, hoping to transform into anyone but myself, as if to be reborn with a new life, thereby overcoming all my negative feelings toward myself. To be fair, it did help, but not entirely. Possibly my trauma was far too deep to be recovered from, at least not simply with foundation or powder.

'I'm teaching a make-up class this Saturday,' I told Chris.

'You started working part-time?' he asked. 'Since when?'

'Just for this Saturday. I'm acting as a guest teacher.'

'I didn't know you teach.'

'I do it once in a while.'

'Can I come?' He grinned.

'If you come, I don't think the students will pay any attention to me. I might as well just go home and take a nap.' I laughed.

'Okay, but where is it?'

'It's near King's Cross Station.' I paused, feeling a bit sceptical. 'Why? Why do you need to know?'

'Just asking.'

'Promise me you're not coming.'

'Will you be wearing glasses when you teach?' He ignored my request and asked an absurd question.

'Yes, but why...' As I spoke, I noticed his gaze dropped down to my cleavage. Knowing he must be having some kind of erotic fantasy, I threw him a punch. 'You dirty devil.'

He caught my hand and pulled my body to him. 'You know ... I never see you in glasses...' he said as he crushed his lips on mine, sending me to his love island.

On Saturday, I took a final check on my case to ensure I had all the teaching equipment. Before I left the flat, I double-checked my outfit – a black T-shirt, black trousers and black-framed glasses. Perfect for a tutor.

I arrived at the studio fifteen minutes early to set up my stuff for the lesson.

Soon after, the students arrived. I was informed that the class was full and I should expect more than had reserved. I was fine with that since I would mostly be demonstrating the procedures, so it didn't matter how many people were attending.

All seats were taken before the class started and some students even had to stand.

I scanned through the crowded room, glimpsing the sea of students, and that was when I noticed a man – a man I would never have imagined seeing here.

Oh my God, what is he doing here?

Derek was wearing black from head to toe and sat quietly in the last row near the exit. I stood there gawking at him, thinking of all the possible reasons for him to be sitting there.

Perhaps he came to learn. But learn from me?

I guessed my gaze on him was slightly too long; some of my students turned around to check who I was looking at.

Not sure whether Derek would want to be seen, I started the lesson promptly so the students didn't have time to look around the room.

It is hard to stay focused when someone who has messed with your mind is sitting opposite you, but as time went by, my nerves gradually lessened. Eventually, I forgot about Derek's appearance and focused on teaching.

The students knuckled down – well, of course, they had paid three hundred pounds for this two-hour lesson. Usually, I would have a short Q&A after each section, just as a wrap-up before going on to the next part.

'Are there any questions so far?' I asked after I finished teaching eye make-up.

A girl in the front row raised her hand. 'Which famous people have you worked with?'

That question was kind of unrelated to the lesson, but I'd got used to it as newbies always focused on celebrities. Once they had worked with them long enough, they wouldn't feel a damn thing.

'There've been a lot.' I smiled. 'Katie Queen, Lisa M, Jo Brad ... et cetera.'

I saw the admiring gazes of the students when I said the names of the celebrities, but they didn't know yet that these celebrities were a pain in the ass.

'How about Chris Steward?' someone at the back shouted, and I happened to recognise the voice.

All the students looked at me, waiting for my

confirmation. No matter how reluctant I was, I nodded. I didn't want to lie.

The audience gasped with surprise.

'If there are no further questions, let's move on to the next section.' I quickly switched to the next topic. I didn't want anyone to ask any weird questions, especially *someone* in the back row.

When I finally finished the two hours of teaching, the students clapped as a thank-you gesture. I nodded to the audience and quickly concluded.

Before the class left, students queued up to ask questions of their own, mostly about how to enter the industry, or if I could introduce them to the industry. It took me an extra thirty minutes to satisfy them, and when I was done, the classroom was empty.

I took a breath and slowly packed my stuff.

A man's voice spoke from behind me. 'I didn't know you worked with Lisa M.'

I already knew the owner of the voice. Without lifting my eyes, I said, 'Yeah, I worked with her a couple of times.' I turned around and was met with a sparkling black gaze. Our eyes locked, and we both flashed a smile at each other.

'What the hell are you doing here?' I laughed.

'No hug?' Derek laughed and opened his arms.

I looked at him, a bit hesitant as Chris's face flashed in my head.

'He banned you from giving me a hug?' He smirked.

'What?'

'Come on, do you think I didn't notice you two.'

His words raised an alert. I quickly checked whether there were other people around. But no one except for me and Derek was in the room. I secretly let out a breath.

'I don't know what you're talking about.' I still didn't want to admit it to him.

'Fine.' He sighed. 'So how have you been lately? I've been trying to reach you but I guess you're busy.'

'Yes, I am kind of busy.' I felt guilty since I was hiding the truth from him. 'Wait a minute, how come you're here?' I squinted.

He laughed and scratched his head. 'I saw your Instagram so I knew you were teaching today.'

'You came here to learn make-up?' I laughed. 'Can't you just hire a make-up artist?'

'I haven't come to learn, I've come to talk to you.'

'You can just call me.' I laughed but quickly realised I was the one who hadn't answered his calls.

'Yes, but you're busy.' He flashed me a smile, one that told me he knew I was avoiding him.

'Derek…' I tried to think of an excuse but when I saw the sincerity in his eyes, I felt sorry for lying to him. 'I'm sorry.'

He looked at my culpable face and nodded. 'I thought so.'

'He thought you liked me, that's why he was mad about me seeing you.' I sent him a sheepish smile, hoping he would forgive my rudeness. 'I've already told him you're my good friend, but he didn't buy it and has some kind of crazy imagination.'

'Good friend?' Derek raised a brow. 'You just broke my heart.' He smiled.

'Huh?'

'After all the things I did, I'm just a good friend?'

'What do you mean?'

'I like you, Anna. Can't you feel it?' He moved closer to me.

'But Derek…'

Before I could finish the sentence, Derek pulled me to his chest and wrapped his arms around my waist. His movement was so fast that I couldn't react. 'Haven't you felt it all these years?' he whispered in my ear.

His confession froze my body and bombed my brain. I should have pushed him off right away, but I didn't want to hurt a friend. While I was thinking of the best rejection line, a voice spoke.

'Anna?'

Derek and I both looked towards the door and saw someone I didn't expect to see.

'Chris!' I screamed as I quickly pushed Derek away. 'It's not what you think.' I walked over to him and grabbed his arm. I could see the anger in his eyes but I didn't know how to comfort him at that moment. I just had to stand there and wait for the flame to burn out.

'He's just toying with you, Anna,' Derek said. 'If you knew his reputation you would have run away.'

'What do you mean?' I frowned; his words raised a suspicion. 'What reputation?'

'Yeah, what's better than made-up lies to rule out your competitor.' Chris grinned. 'I don't have time for this.' He looked at me and pointed his head to the lift. 'Let's go.' He turned around and left.

I looked at his back and then at Derek, feeling guilty and regretful for not recognising his feelings before. If I had known earlier, none of this would have happened.

'I am sorry.' I tried to steady my gaze on Derek, but my guilt had me breaking our eye contact. I grabbed my stuff and chased after Chris, leaving Derek alone in the room. I caught up to Chris and wanted to walk with him side by side, but I was scared of his angry stare. So I walked behind him like a little puppy.

After we got into the car, I took a peek at him, but his face was not readable. Without saying a word, he started the engine and drove off.

My mind flew to when he first knew about Derek. I had a feeling the same sleepless night would happen again.

Depression quickly fell on me. We had just made up and everything was back on track, but with the incident today, my efforts had once again vanished like steam.

I began to plan for the explanation, but I didn't think he would believe a word I said.

He would be leaving me. I was positive about that.

When we arrived in the car park both of us stayed still, and neither of us got out of the car. I knew I needed to settle this right here.

I decided to tell the truth, and if he didn't believe me, there was nothing more I could do. 'You are right. Derek does like me,' I said.

Chris remained silent and I was too afraid to look at him.

'I didn't invite him to the class,' I added, hoping Chris would at least give me a slight reaction so I knew what to say next.

After a minute of silence, he finally spoke. 'It's your Instagram, right?'

'What?'

'He found out your class time and location on Instagram, right?'

I was so relieved when he said that; at least I knew he might believe my explanation of what happened.

'Yes, he said he couldn't reach me so he came in person.'

As I turned my head to face him, I realised his gaze was already locked on me, not in anger but full of tenderness.

'You have been ignoring his calls?'

I nodded.

He slowly took my hand to his lips. 'Okay.' He landed a kiss on the back of the hand.

'You're not angry?'

'Do I need to be angry?' He smirked.

'No, but you believe I didn't invite him?'

'Did you invite him?'

'No! But that's not my point.'

He laughed. 'It's funny when you try so hard to explain.' He slid his finger across my cheek. 'If I can find you through Instagram, so can others, right?'

'You looked for me on Instagram?'

'Yeah, because you wouldn't tell me where you were teaching your class,' he argued, 'and I really wanted to see you in glasses.' He grinned with a twinkle in his eye.

I sent a soft punch to his arm.

The next day, I received a text from Derek, asking whether we could meet again. He wanted to explain himself about yesterday.

I wanted to meet him, but to apologise for what had happened. Not only because he was a well-respected director in the industry, but also because he was my friend. I also feared that having a bad relationship with him would affect Chris's career.

I hesitated about whether I should tell Chris because I was pretty sure he would ban me from seeing him. Yet I knew I had to do this, even though he would resent it. In the end, I decided to see Derek in secret.

'Hey, I need to pop by the cosmetic store – I ran out of

foundation.' After I finished styling Chris, I found a gap to sneak out.

'Will you come back to the studio?'

'No, I'll meet you at home.'

Before I left the room, Chris pulled me to his chest and gave me a peck on my lips.

The tenderness in his eyes sent me to guilty land. I felt bad for hiding a secret from him, yet I had no choice.

Derek was already at the café when I arrived.

'Just coffee,' I said to the waiter.

I glanced at the clock on the wall and ran my script through my head one more time. Today must be the day to solve our misunderstandings quickly and quietly.

'Derek—'

'I'm sorry about yesterday,' he said.

'I should be the one to apologise.' I tilted my head. 'I'm not very bright, you see.'

'No, you're smart.' Derek softened his gaze. 'You just didn't have your attention on me.'

His confession of his feelings once again made me uncomfortable. I had always treated him like a friend, or even a brother, and it sent a shiver down my spine when I listened to how he felt about me.

'Derek, I—'

'No need to say sorry.' He laughed. 'I know.'

'So can we be friends again?' I smiled.

My expectation was a smile and a nod, and then everything would be solved. But things turned out differently.

He sank into silence for a while, as if hesitating whether to spill out a secret.

'Or not?' I joked, trying to relieve the tension, but it was useless.

'How much do you know about him?'

He had turned the conversation back to my relationship with Chris. But I didn't want to share my feelings with him. In fact, I would have liked to keep everything in the dark.

'Enough,' I said, keeping my answer simple.

Derek laughed and looked out of the window. When his gaze returned to me, he leaned forward. 'He is not what you think.'

His bad-mouthing Chris made my nerves jump, in a negative way, especially since I was sure I knew him better than anyone. It was not fair to Chris that people could judge and make assumptions based merely on some unverified gossip. I felt an overwhelming urge to slam the table and walk away, but I would achieve nothing if I ended the meeting right now. My rational sense won and put my anger to sleep. In just a few seconds, I cooled off and displayed a weird, reluctant smile. 'Derek, I know you care about me…'

'How long have you been with him?' He ignored my words and continued questioning me about my personal life.

'Almost a year,' I said. 'I know him well enough.'

Derek tutted. 'Do you know he changes girlfriends annually? We call him "never a year"…'

Pain spread through my forehead like a bullet had been fired into my skull.

If Derek's idea was to kill me, he had succeeded. But I guess he hadn't finished because he was about to drag me to hell to complete the job.

'He just dumps girls when he gets bored. He avoids them or ignores them, so the girls get the hint and finally leave on their own. Always a clean break-up, no mess left behind,' he said.

His words were like a bomb exploding inside me. My assassination was complete.

The waiter came over and placed my drink on the table. I looked at the steamy coffee, and my mouth tasted the bitterness before I'd even taken a sip.

'Derek.' I released a breath and tried to calm myself before saying anything I might regret. I didn't want to make things worse by having an angry conversation; they never end well. 'I know him better than anyone.'

'Anna...'

'Please.' I needed to stop him from further insulting my boyfriend. 'I understand what you mean, but I will take my chances.'

Derek stared at me; the black gaze was covered with fog, totally unreadable.

'I don't expect you will forgive me, but I really hope my relationship with Chris won't affect our friendship,' I said.

Derek sighed deeply as he shook his head. 'Anna, I'm always here for you, no matter what.'

I was grateful for his kindness, but I could only return my friendship to him.

We updated each other regarding life and work; he didn't hold a grudge and still welcomed me as a friend after that embarrassing situation.

Our chat was fun and fruitful, and we went our separate ways when Derek received a client dinner notification.

'I'll still see you around, huh?' he asked.

'Of course. We should do more gatherings.' I laughed.

'Only if your boyfriend allows you.' He smirked.

When I got home, Chris had already returned.

Snowball ran to me as usual, asking for petting.

I stroked his fur and kissed him. 'Good boy.'

The lovely smell of food attracted my attention. I walked to the kitchen where Chris was cooking dinner.

Chris saw me when he turned around. 'You're back! Steak night.'

I walked over to hug him and kiss him. 'Thank you so much,' I said.

'Can you help me to set the table?'

After I finished, he came over with two plates of steak.

Like a waiter, he laid down a plate in front of me. 'Medium rare.'

The dry-aged rib-eye was amazingly soft and juicy, and I held up a thumb to credit him.

After dinner, I took a shower while Chris took care of Snowball and had some playtime with him.

It had been a long but rewarding day. When I thought my relationship with Derek might be ended, his mature attitude saved our friendship.

His confession of his feelings was uncomfortable, but we had got over it and were now as usual. Despite the feelings he had for me, he was a dear friend, a great listener and an adviser. He taught me different aspects of work, especially communication with co-workers, how to deal with troubled celebrities, and satisfying the boss without crossing the line.

Never a year.

His words flashed in my head, and once again left me deflated.

What if everything he said was true?

I never googled Chris's past relationship because from

what I knew, ninety per cent of the rumours were fake, five per cent were maybe true, and the other five per cent were half true. But I didn't ask Chris in person either because everyone has an unwanted past. I believed the future we built together would be far more crucial.

My mind seemed to be whirling in strong rapids and drowning in a sea of worries and disappointment. Maybe instead of going crazy in the shower, I should ask him directly to ease my concern.

When I got out of the bathroom, Chris seemed to be nowhere in the house.

I walked around and realised he was still in the kitchen.

'Chris?' I smiled, drying my hair with a small towel.

Chris had his back to me and was leaning on the kitchen island; he didn't turn around when I called his name. I walked closer and noticed my phone was on the island table.

'Hey, you can use the bathroom now.' I searched the room to find our roommate. 'Where is Snowball?'

'Where did you go today?' Chris still had his back to me.

'What do you mean?'

He turned around and locked his gaze on me; that unreadable face had returned. My sensitive instinct told me something had happened.

'After the last job, where did you go today?' Anger lingered in his voice.

'I don't understand.'

Chris let out a breath, eyes full of disgust.

'Did you get a receipt for the foundation?'

I finally realised what might have caused him outrage, but how did he know?

A buzzing sound on the island table caught my attention;

my mobile kept vibrating with notifications. When I brought it close to check the message, I realised the phone was unlocked. I wanted to applaud my Sherlock instinct because I had just solved the mystery behind his anger.

'You've checked my phone?' I barked.

'Can you tell me where your receipt is?'

My rage level immediately went from five to ten. 'How can you—'

'You lied to me about going to buy foundation and went to meet your boyfriend.' Chris's gaze sparkled with flame. 'How many times have you lied to me?'

'What?' I was surprised by his words. How could he suspect my loyalty? Besides, I was doing it not only because of my friendship with Derek but also for his sake. How could he?

'I was not secretly meeting Derek, if that's what you're implying. Also, this is my last reminder that he is not my boyfriend, he's just a friend.' I raised my voice, and in the end, I was almost shouting.

Animals always had the best survival instincts. Snowball was hiding behind a wall. He looked at us with his big round eyes, yet he didn't come close. He probably knew it was better to observe than run to the war zone right now.

'If there's nothing to hide, why did you lie to me in the first place?'

'Like you will happily let me go to meet him?' I said sarcastically, rolling my eyes.

'If you know I don't like it, then why are you still meeting him? Why are you doing things that I hate?'

I felt totally defeated. I had no energy to argue with him further. 'I did it for the sake of both of us,' I said weakly. 'Yes,

I met him because I don't want to lose a friend like him. But you also have to understand that he is not someone you want to mess with.' I approached him slowly. 'I know you're already a top actor, but he is also a well-respected director. I was trying to fix what was damaged. I am not asking you to talk to him or kowtow to him.'

'So what have you exchanged with him? A night?'

My stomach twisted.

His words were like millions of icicles falling at high speed and stabbing right into my heart. I looked at him, speechless, lips trembling and tears filling my eyes. My anger had turned into a deep disappointment. Never had I imagined he would say something so heartbreaking.

'Nothing.' My voice was quavering. But my pride wouldn't let me break down right now. 'Believe it or not, he's a decent person. He might like me, but that doesn't make him a monster.'

I glanced down to the floor because I knew my tears could no longer be held back. They had to come right now. I felt a wet touch on my leg. I looked to the side and saw Snowball sitting next to me. He put out one paw to touch my lower leg. His warm gesture made my tears escape even faster.

I lowered my body to the floor and hugged him tight. 'Thank you.'

After a long silence, Chris spoke. 'You know what your problem is? You never tell me anything.'

I glued my gaze to the floor because I didn't want him to see my torn eyes.

Chris let out a breath and then he kneeled before me. 'Look at me.' He grabbed my shoulder and forced my body to turn to him. I reluctantly lifted my chin. When our gazes locked, he cupped my face in his hand. 'I should be the one protecting you, not the other way round.'

I wanted to argue with him but he held a finger to my lips and stopped me from saying anything further.

'I don't need your protection, Anna.' He leaned over and kissed me. 'I just need your love.'

CHAPTER SEVEN

It was Chris's father's birthday on Sunday and they had invited me to the party.

I was even more nervous than before because I would be attending as Chris's girlfriend.

Not that it was much of a big deal, but I wanted to leave a good impression. The day before his birthday, I decided to go to the shops to find a suitable gift.

'I can't eat with you tonight,' I said to Chris when we were alone in the dressing room.

'Going somewhere?' he asked with a sceptical look.

After the meeting with Derek a couple of weeks ago, he had become a little clingy. He asked my whereabouts whenever I was out of his sight, even for just a while. He would drive me everywhere but wouldn't leave me alone.

'I'm going to Harvey Nichols to get your father a gift,' I replied with a smile, trying to cover whatever emotion I felt.

Practice makes perfect; after a few weeks of training, I had successfully passed his test.

'Sure.' Chris relaxed his eyebrows. 'I will drive you there after we finish the shoot today.'

I nodded with a fake smile on my face.

We went shopping after the shoot.

'What are you getting for my father?' Chris asked when he pulled his car to the side of the road. 'Just curious,' he added with a smile.

'Not sure, I might get him...' I paused before the word 'whisky' popped out of my mouth. I didn't want to remind him of Derek and start a silent fight tonight. 'A tie?'

'Good choice. You might want to try one of those with funny patterns.'

'Funny patterns?'

'Yes, like the Simpsons, a cat or even doughnuts.'

'I know what you mean.' I laughed. 'I might be a while – do you want to go home? I could grab an Uber.'

'Just go,' he said as he dropped a kiss on my cheek.

I walked into the shop and unconsciously let out a breath; the suffocating pressure on my chest was immediately relieved. I looked at the tie department where a cute-looking salesman was fixing a tie rack and putting the products straight. I was sure that pretty boy could pick the right tie for me in five seconds, and then Chris wouldn't need to wait too long in the car. But thinking of the tension I would have with him in the car, my subconscious had me walking towards the other side of the department store, heading to the chocolate counter instead.

A pretty young lady came over. 'Good evening, may I help you?'

'Thank you, but I would like to look around first.'

'Sure, just let me know when you need help.' She returned to the cash desk.

I walked around the shop and browsed the chocolate descriptions – mint flavour, orange flavour, strawberry flavour. I was reading the words, but none sank in.

The first week when I felt the change in Chris, I was confused. Before the incident, he liked to hang out all the time, but he still gave me plenty of personal space. Sometimes he would go out for dinner with friends or family alone. But now he would only go out with me or we would stay at home. It felt like having a twenty-four-hour bodyguard.

Once, I read in a magazine that one of the readers cheated on her husband. Then she needed to report her location to her husband every hour after her affair was exposed. Obviously, there was a trust issue between them, but I'd never cheated, so why was I treated like I had?

'This is our best-selling ruby chocolate. Would you like to try it?'

The sales lady was holding a silver plate with a few pink chocolate blocks placed neatly in a line. I took one and the sweetness overtook me, but instead of it bringing happiness, I felt tired and depressed. The sugar high never came as expected.

I left the chocolate store and went back to the tie shop. As predicted, the salesman picked a smiley cow tie in less than five seconds; the style was spot on.

'You've got the tie?' Chris asked when I got in the car.

'Yep, I want your father to smile whenever he drinks milk.'

Chris chuckled. 'You bought a cow tie?'

I nodded.

'Cheeky.' He pulled my hand to his lips.

The touch of his lips still gave me an electric shock. I

watched this handsome man focus on driving, and a mixture of feelings built in me.

We went back home and as I was about to go in the shower, Chris pulled my arm. 'Anna, I'm sorry,' he said.

The sudden apology astonished me. I looked at him with wide eyes. 'Why?' I asked.

'I know I've been a pain in the ass these last few weeks.' He smiled.

Though I wanted to deny it, I found it difficult to lie. Like an idiot, I just stared at him, open-mouthed.

'I see you agree with me.' He smirked.

I sighed, not knowing what to say.

'But it's not my fault, you know?' Chris's gaze locked with mine. I guessed he saw the spark of anger in my eyes, and he added before I could speak, 'I don't know you. I never did.'

'What do you mean? You know where I live, what my job is, my family status.'

'Yes, but you never told me that stuff. I only found out from others. There are secrets after secrets...' Chris paused with a sheepish smile. 'After all this time, you are still a stranger to me.'

I had never seen such tenderness in his gaze, not in real life or in any character he had played. I watched this beautiful man; his sincerity gave me mixed feelings of pressure and love all at once. The fact that he could change my emotions like flicking a switch scared me, and I felt like a puppet in his hand.

The next day, after work, we went to Chris's father's house. When we arrived, it was almost 6 p.m.

As usual, his mother came out of the house to greet us. 'Anna.' She hugged me tight with a bright smile. 'I missed you.'

'Me too.' I smiled.

'Glad you didn't flee from his boat.' Chris's father walked toward us laughing.

'Dad!' Chris rolled his eyes. 'You just had to make a scene.' They happily hugged each other.

When I walked into the house, it was filled with the scent of turkey and beef. My hunger alarm was awakened immediately by this delicious savoury aroma.

'Anna.' A boy ran to me with a smiley face, but too fast and bumped his head on my leg. 'I missed you.'

'Hello, Ben.' I kneeled and hugged him. 'I missed you too.'

He looked up and stared at me in silence.

'What's wrong, Ben?' I asked.

He shook his head and pulled me to the dinner table to sit with him.

Everyone was seated when dinner was ready. The table was filled with turkey, beef brisket and mashed potato, and this wonderful dinner was paired with bottles of white and red wine.

'Cheers.' Our glasses gently clinked with one another, forming the most beautiful crystal sound.

'Happy birthday, Dad,' everyone shouted.

Cosy, warm and festive. It was a joy that I had never encountered, or perhaps I had once but it was left in the past.

I watched the family and a sense of jealousy rose from

nowhere – it was the warmth that everyone should have but I could only watch on TV.

A warm hand gently touched mine. I followed the hand and met Chris's gaze. The sincerity in his eyes told me he understood the struggle I was having.

I looked away with shame. I was disgusted by my bad thoughts.

'Anna.' Ben looked at me seriously, but with that baby face, the cautious look became very funny.

'Yes?' I hid my smile behind a serious face. 'What's wrong?'

He shot me a glance, then he pulled out a candy ring. 'Will you marry me?'

A pause floated in the air, and the next second everyone broke into laughter.

'Ben!' His mother laughed with tears in her eyes. 'You know she's dating Uncle Chris.'

'I know,' Ben shouted; his cheeks were red. 'But Uncle Chris changes girlfriends all the time anyway.'

'Hey!' Chris laughed. 'You can't say that here! Not in front of my girlfriend.'

Everyone laughed, me too, but with a Barbie-type plastic smile.

Never a year.

Derek's words once again flashed before my mind. Would he really break up with me one day? End of story?

'Don't take his words seriously,' Chris's dad said. 'He likes to make up stuff.'

'No, I...' Ben stopped speaking as he saw the warning eyes of his mother.

He turned his little head and furiously punched his fork into his potato.

In the meantime, I dived into my thoughts, playing all scenarios of being dumped by Chris. I guess I was too busy imagining myself to be an actress with a sad ending, I failed to hear the question from Angela.

'What?' I asked, confused.

Angela gave me a rictus smile.

Did she say something important?

I peeked at Chris, and he also seemed dejected.

'I was asking—' Angela was about to say something, but Chris's father interrupted.

'If you and Chris planned to get married?'

His question blanked out my mind.

I never thought about marrying him, because it was already hard to keep our relationship together. Marriage seemed too far for us.

'I never really thought about that.' I peeked at Chris. He was emotionless and unreadable.

'Well, they are still young.' Clare broke the embarrassment.

Chris's brother swiftly changed the subject and began to talk about the boat he bought last week.

Everyone turned their attention to him. I glanced at Chris, and he returned the gaze. When I thought he looked a bit disappointed, he flashed me a smile.

My memory flew back to the idea of him dumping me.

I tried to convince myself it would be fine; we would be fine. I wore a smile on my face but was not able to enjoy my food.

The dinner ended wonderfully; everyone was cheerful and a bit drunk. I think Chris had had one or two strong drinks – he seemed a bit tipsy.

'Let's get an Uber,' he said as he switched on the app. 'You take the first one and I'll take the one after, okay?'

It was not a big deal calling different Ubers because we were trying to hide our secret from everyone except his family, and I was the one who demanded this. Like a perfect boyfriend, he was just dancing along, satisfying my awkward and insecure request. But after what Ben had said tonight, anything, however minor, made my nerves jump.

He wants a separate Uber now and perhaps a separate life later?

Was that a clue for me to get a life?

Why did he agree not to go public in the first place?

Travelling separately should have fitted well into our hiding-in-the-closet scenario, yet the uncertainty that came from this secretiveness once again confused my already sceptical mind. This tiny incident immediately forced thousands of questions into my head. *How pathetic!* I wish I wasn't always so diplomatic and had the courage to speak the truth sometimes.

When I got in the Uber, I began to wonder whether I should go to his place or an Airbnb. I needed to cool down my mixed-up head before I said anything that I would regret.

I sank into my thoughts so deeply that I was unaware of my whereabouts, not until the corner of my eye caught a glimpse of a familiar building. My heart dropped as I realised my Uber driver had efficiently brought me to Chris's apartment.

If you want to leave, anytime from now would be good.

While my mind struggled to make a decision, my body decided to follow its own will and get out of the car to wait for a further signal. Like a mannequin without a mind of its own, I looked blank and stood still in front of the building.

'What are you standing there for?' Chris gently patted my shoulder, whispering in my ear.

His sudden appearance scared me to hell. 'You've arrived?' I smiled as a cover-up. 'I was just waiting for you.'

'Sure.' He looked behind him as he spoke, and when he confirmed no one was around, he indicated the apartment lobby. 'Next time, you might want to wait inside.' He turned his back and walked straight into the building, leaving me with a forced smile and millions of questions in my head.

Chris and I were woken by Snowball's licking attack. We both got out of bed and dressed in a hurry as we were late for the 7 a.m. call.

'Do you want to grab an Uber today? I don't think there's time for you to walk one stop to the location,' Chris said while putting on his shirt.

Usually, Chris would drive and drop me off half a mile before the destination to avoid people seeing us together. But today we seemed to be very late, so I agreed.

While I was checking the inventory in my case, Chris received a call. He glanced at the screen but instead of hanging up, he muted the ringtone.

'You are not answering it?' I asked.

Chris paused a second before saying, 'It's just some property salespeople.'

'You're thinking of buying another place?'

He glanced at me without answering.

Before I could tease him about his suspicious look, he turned his back on me, blocking my view of his face.

'No, they're just fishing for a new client.'

I stared at his back, feeling a bit depressed. His cold attitude made me feel as if he was building a wall between us. The problem was I didn't know what had happened – had I said something or done something? Was it Derek? But he hadn't been around since that make-up class; we should have made up on that topic.

I hated it when I didn't know what the problem was, just flying blind to try to solve it.

'Your Uber is here.' He walked to the entrance and opened the door. 'See you later.' He shut the door on me without kissing me goodbye.

He always kissed me before I left.

I stood in the lift lobby and looked resignedly at the shut door, mixed feelings crawling through my mind.

I hoped it was just my insecurity that had led to an overreaction. I persuaded myself not to question Chris on every little action; it would not only drive both of us crazy but also open an endless road of suspicion.

No matter how reluctant I was, I forced myself to leave the flat, facing the fact that my question would not be solved today, at least not for now. Maybe Chris would return to normal later. Artistic people were often moody and emotional, and I should know it better than most. It was just one of those days, I told myself.

After I got into the Uber, I asked the driver to stop by a café so I could get breakfast for Chris and myself.

When I arrived at the location, Chris's car was already in the car park.

I followed the directions provided by the staff and headed to Chris's changing room. The door was half open. As I reached for the doorknob, a voice spoke from inside the room.

'I like you…' A woman giggled. 'How about you come over tonight and we can get to know each other?' My heart pounded.

Who was the woman talking to?

'Sounds intriguing,' a familiar voice replied.

My mood dropped when I recognised Chris's voice.

While I was deciding whether I should storm in or leave, the woman spoke again. 'Yes, it is…'

Her voice was so soft and I could imagine she was making the most seductive face to Chris.

'But no, it's not appropriate.' Chris laughed in a sexy low tone.

'Oh…' Her voice dropped, sounding disappointed. 'Why?'

'Well…'

'You have a girlfriend?' she asked.

'Unfortunately, nope,' Chris said.

I knew I was the one who decided not to go public, yet his answer was like a knife stabbing into my heart.

'Then what's stopping you?'

'Because…'

I stormed in without further thought because I'd heard enough. I didn't want to hear one more lie from him.

'Hey, you're here early!' I smiled at Chris.

Just as I thought, the woman had her hand on Chris's chest. The chest that I lay on this morning. I buried my feelings in my guts and pulled up the most friendly face I had to cover my anger. I needed to hide my emotions not only from that woman but also from Chris.

The woman kept her hand on his chest even after my appearance, just as if she didn't care if anyone witnessed her passion for Chris.

'I'll see you later, Chris.' She slid her fingers off his chest. Chris returned an evil smile.

After she left, I started setting up the make-up panel.

'You're late,' Chris said. 'Where have you been?' he asked casually as if nothing had happened, as if what I had heard and seen was just an acting job.

'To the café.' I had my back to him and tried to soothe my anger before facing him. 'Who was she?' I asked calmly. Each word and tone was carefully planned. I didn't want to give any hint of my anger.

'Some supermodel, I guess,' he mumbled.

I turned my head and saw that he was playing on his phone, not taking any of my words seriously.

'She seems to be interested in you.' I forced out a smile at him.

He stopped typing on the phone and tilted his head up, locking his gaze on me. I thought he would give me that evil grin, but instead, he returned his focus to the screen. 'She's no one.'

I wanted to chase the answer further but his phone rang. He took a glimpse at the screen and his brow lifted, screaming excitement. But the next second he calmed down and took a peek at me. When he caught my eye, he quickly looked down at his phone, not giving any explanation.

'Another property sale?' I grinned.

'Just some friends.' This time he didn't even bother to look up and continued texting whomever it was.

I could no longer withhold my emotion; the silent game was never my strongest thing.

'What's the matter, Chris?' I asked.

'What do you mean?'

'You're acting strange.'

'No, I'm not.' He sighed. 'Don't overthink stuff, okay?'

He came over and kissed me on my forehead. 'Don't we need to prepare for the shoot now?'

His kiss didn't reassure me, but this was not the right time or place to discuss anything. I nodded and decided to leave this issue to another day.

'Gosh, I need a break,' I screamed.

After thirteen hours of non-stop working for three weeks, I was worn out. I had no words to describe my tiredness; I was not only physically tired but also mentally sick. The people I worked with were demanding and annoying; to be able to work with them I had to put on a tough face. But I was working with my boyfriend, work romance, oh, how sweet!

Wrong! There was nothing romantic about working with Chris; he wouldn't be kind if any mistake was made, and he even scolded me a couple of times in front of the crew. I didn't blame him, because I'd made the mistake, but sometimes I wondered whether that level of anger was necessary. To avoid getting scolded again, I needed to be extremely careful about everything.

Imagine how tiring it is when you have to stay alert all the time.

'Stop whining,' Chris teased. 'We just have one more shoot for today.'

He tried on the black leather jacket given to him by the sponsor and pulled the zip up, hiding his perfect figure.

While he was fiddling with his sleeves, I couldn't help

but watch his perfect body. I guessed he felt my stare, so he looked up and met my gaze. The black leather he was wearing brought out his olive eyes, so they were even greener. I felt like diving into the green ocean.

We held our stare for a few seconds, but instead of planting a kiss on me as usual, Chris looked away and turned his back on me.

'Can you get me the scarf? It should be in the bag,' he said.

I was a bit relieved that he had turned away because I didn't want to let him see the disappointment in my eyes.

His cold, distant attitude had appeared since dinner with his family; each time he looked away or kept silent would lead me to second-guess myself – had I said or done something unpleasant? Not once did I get an answer, and just ended up screaming inside my head *What is it this time?*

In the beginning, I thought he just didn't want to mix romance with work, but even when we were alone at home, he seemed to be avoiding me.

'Hey, wanna go to your friend's restaurant for dinner tonight?' I asked, thinking I should give it a shot by making the first move.

'Who?' Chris frowned, thinking hard. 'Oh, Richard?'

Finally, it rang a bell.

I nodded as I passed him the scarf he wanted.

He wrapped it around his neck. The dark green wool enhanced the softness of his eyes.

'Sure, but I need to go somewhere first.' He looked in the mirror and adjusted the length of the scarf. When he was done he looked at me through the mirror. 'I'll meet you at the restaurant, okay?'

I returned my gaze to him through the mirror and gave

him a nod. Before I could flash him a smile, he'd already returned his focus to the scarf.

A buzz on my phone drew my attention. The screen popped up a familiar name, Derek.

Bad timing!

I muted the call and pretended to be busy.

'You're not answering it?' Chris asked and looked at me through the mirror.

I was caught off guard because I was busy thinking about both his cold attitude and the call.

'Later, just a friend,' I said without thinking, and now I wanted to bite my tongue.

He stared into my eyes and at that moment he already knew who the caller was. When I thought he was about to fire up, he just calmly said, 'Okay.' There were no follow-up questions or angry stares; he was completely emotionless.

'Let's go, I think we need to be at studio one now.' He opened the door and signalled me to go first. 'Come on, I don't want to be late.' He sounded like my boss. Well, he was my boss.

After the shoot, I headed back to the changing room and began packing my stuff.

I was tired and hungry. The gurgling in my belly stimulated my brain and flashed images of a juicy burger in my head. I advanced from hungry to starving.

Chris came into the changing room. 'Hey, I'll see you later.'

I gave him a nod and off he went.

Was I curious about where he was going? Of course. My 'Sherlock' instinct wanted to chase him for the answer. But I didn't like to pry.

My Uber arrived after I finished packing my case.

'To the pub, right,' the driver asked.

'Yes.'

'You work for this magazine?' the driver casually asked after ten minutes of driving.

'Not really, just working on a project with them.' I didn't want to say too much about my work to someone I didn't know.

'Did you see any celebrities today?'

I laughed; maybe that was what people thought when they knew someone was in this industry.

'Not really.' I didn't want to get him too excited because I needed a driver that would focus on driving.

'Oh.' He sounded disappointed but had his focus on the wheel rather than on me.

After five minutes of silence, he spoke again. 'It's a bit chilly today,' he said in a voice that sounded like he was mumbling to himself.

'Yes. I guess autumn is coming.' I looked out of the window, thinking about Chris and how he denied having a girlfriend today. But that wasn't what hurt the most; the way he was avoiding me was killing me.

He was like fire when we were first together, but after the Derek incident, he made me feel like a prisoner, and after the family dinner, he'd been as cold as the wind. I had no idea what was going on. I was just like his puppet following his every step.

I wanted to change the situation, but I was powerless.

Maybe my sadness had infected the car; the Uber driver didn't talk anymore until we arrived. 'Here we are,' he said.

'Thanks.' I opened the car door and stepped outside.

'Hey...' He spoke again before I closed the door. 'Don't

lose hope, the weather should be better tomorrow.' He flashed me a smile.

I squinted, confused about his words, but the next second I realised he was trying to cheer me up. My depressed face must have been so obvious.

'Yeah, I hope so.' I smiled back and watched him drive off.

When I got into the pub, Richard came over to welcome me. We had a brief chit-chat and he led me to our usual private seat.

I checked my email on my phone, there were just some work notes for the coming week and an email from my boss. I quickly replied to her and finished my work for the day.

Thirty minutes passed, but there was no sign of Chris. My tummy began to play the drums so I ordered.

When the meal arrived, Chris was still a no-show, so I texted him to see whether he was okay.

He replied that he needed a couple of minutes, so I began my meal without him. But he hadn't shown up when I finished the last of the chips.

While I was wondering if he had forgotten about me, my phone beeped. Apparently, he still hadn't finished whatever he was doing. I told him not to worry and that I would go home.

Richard came over and passed me the bill. 'He didn't show up?'

'He's busy.' I forced out a smile. 'The burger was delicious.' It was better to change the subject before I started whining about how Chris had treated me lately. Richard was not the person I would go to for girls' talk.

'I'm glad you liked it,' he said as he escorted me out. 'Next time he comes, I will kick his ass.'

I laughed and waved him goodbye.

When I arrived home, Snowball jumped on me.

'Snowball!' I giggled while he licked my face.

The smile on his face swept all my depression away.

'Okay, okay.' I walked over to the kitchen and looked for his treats. When I took out the plastic bag, the sound of the wrapper got him excited. He stood up tall with two legs trying to reach the bag I was holding.

'You're standing up!' I laughed and took out my phone to capture this funny scene.

A couple of shots later, he lost his patience and woofed a reminder to feed him.

'All right, you cute baby.' I happily watched him chew the treat and left all my sadness behind.

The sound of a key jingling came from a distance, probably from outside the flat, but it didn't last long. The door was slammed open. Snowball rushed towards the door but quickly returned to my side. I squinted at his behaviour and decided to walk over to check the entrance. It was Chris. He was leaning on the wall and stumbling towards me. I could smell the alcohol on him wafting over from ten feet away. Obviously, he was drunk.

'Are you okay?' I grabbed his arm.

'Of course!' He laughed and pushed me away.

I had never seen him so drunk; it was as if he had bathed in alcohol. Snowball kept his distance from him.

'Let me take you to the bathroom.' I led him there. This time he didn't push me away.

He went inside and slammed the door closed.

Thirty minutes later, he came out of the bathroom. He said nothing and dropped himself onto the bed. Soon after he fell asleep.

I watched his sleeping back; everything felt unfamiliar and strange.

He was no longer the guy that I knew; that sweet and warm guy had gone.

The next day was Saturday and I woke up without the alarm. When I turned to the side, I could only see the big black eyes of Snowball.

'Hey, morning sweety.' I dropped a kiss on his forehead and looked behind him, but didn't see Chris anywhere.

'He has fed you, huh?' I smiled and dropped another kiss on his head.

Snowball looked at me and took a big stretch.

'You rest a bit longer, huh!' I said to Snowball and went to refresh myself.

When I was done I went to the sitting room where there was no sign of Chris. But then the smell of omelette attracted my attention.

I walked towards the kitchen and found him behind the hob. He wore a white T-shirt and grey joggers. His muscles stretched the T-shirt making it seem too tight for him. I glanced at the shape of his back; every inch of that perfect triangle screamed his efforts in the gym.

'Good morning.' I tried to wipe away my disappointment of last night and acted normal.

Chris turned to me, but quickly dropped his gaze to the hob when our eyes met.

'I've made you an omelette.' He switched off the hob and slid the omelette onto a plate. 'Here you go.'

I beamed at the lovely omelette. I wished this moment could last forever.

Chris sat opposite me with a cup of coffee. He didn't usually eat breakfast to maintain his perfect figure – perhaps even more important when he'd had so much alcohol last night.

I took a peek at him, wondering whether I should start asking questions. But where to begin? Why was he so drunk; who was he with? And why did he stand me up? But I worried that it would turn into a fight, so I hesitated.

Chris suddenly broke the silence. 'I'm sorry about yesterday.'

I looked up and met his olive eyes, but he avoided eye contact and quickly looked down at his coffee. I waited for further explanation but that seemed to be the end of the conversation.

I took another bite of the omelette, and a bitter taste spread over my pallet. I wondered what he had added.

My insecurity was building inside me, the feeling I was losing him was getting strong, yet I was powerless to keep him.

I quietly watched him playing with his phone, but my brain actively concocted an invisible wall between us, and the width of the wall expanded every second. I was just three feet from him, but it felt like miles away.

He looked up at me. 'Are you okay?'

'I'm fine, how about you?' I took this chance, hoping to open his heart. But he said nothing.

'Are you angry with me?' I asked.

He looked down at his coffee and continued the silence.

'Do you want me to leave?'

He swiftly looked up at me. 'No.'

'Chris—'

'Stop overthinking it.' He placed his hand on mine. 'It's not what you think.'

I nodded, but his answer explained nothing.

It was our first anniversary today. But I didn't expect Chris to remember, especially with his weird behaviour lately. That was why I was so surprised when he suggested going on a date with me tonight.

'Hey, I've booked a table for tonight,' he said.

'Really?' I was surprised but felt warm in my heart.

'Yes. I'll meet you in Fountain at seven o'clock, okay? I need to meet someone before that.'

'Fountain is pretty expensive, so you better not stand me up.' I smirked.

He flashed me a sheepish smile. 'I won't.'

The schedule for today was quite quiet; my work shift ended early at 3 p.m. while Chris still needed to work till five. So I decided to go shopping to prepare for tonight's dinner.

My wardrobe didn't contain clothes for a restaurant like Fountain, a three-Michelin-star fine-dining restaurant. I would need a pricey dress, probably from Harvey Nics.

'This red dress looks nice on you,' the assistant from the luxury brand said sincerely.

Yes, it did look good on me, even though I didn't have a curvy figure. The off-shoulder fitted dress made my body look slim but pushed up my flat chest – I went from a B to a D. The magic this dress cast on me made it impossible not to look.

I had already thought of the best hair style for this dress; a messy chignon would go perfectly with the naked neckline. I took out some hairpins and bands and roughly styled my hair, just to confirm my thoughts.

'Wow, I like your hair. You're a stylist?' The assistant shot me an admiring glance.

'Thanks, and yes, I'm a make-up artist.' I smiled as I pinched a few hairs down the side, just to style it loose and natural. 'Do you have any shoes to go with this dress?'

'Of course.' She dashed to the other side of the room to search for a pair of suitable shoes.

I looked at my reflection in the mirror, wondering whether this dress would capture Chris's eyes. It had been a long time since we got together; he had been avoiding me like the plague. Was it because I got fat? But looking at the mirror, my body shape seemed no different and there were no signs of ageing on my face. I leaned closer to the mirror to check for fine lines, but probably my make-up skills were good and they were all covered. I saw nothing but flawless skin.

'Miss, would you like to take a look at these two pairs of shoes?' The assistant appeared in the mirror. I nodded and tried on the shoes.

After thirty minutes of switching between two pairs of shoes, I finally chose the silver wrap sandals.

'Do you need a clutch too?' she asked as she produced two clutch bags.

I looked at the attractive bags and giggled. At this point, I had to applaud this sales assistant, who was not pushy but was upselling me step by step. Amazing.

'I would like the silver one.'

'Good choice, it goes with your shoes.'

I paid for my purchase and headed back home to get ready. Make-up, hair et cetera. After an hour of my makeover, I decided to stop in case I overdid the make-up. I like to keep my make-up light but looking professional.

'What do you think?' I looked in the mirror, admiring my skill at applying light foundation and unnoticeable concealer. The light brown shimmer that spread across my lids softly lifted my eyes. I did not wear any fake lashes because natural was my theme for tonight.

'Woof,' Snowball said.

'Do you think he will like it?' I said.

Snowball tilted his head to the left, looking confused.

'Can't you give me some encouragement?' I laughed and petted his head.

My phone beeped and I knew my Uber was here.

'You will behave, won't you?' I kissed Snowball before heading out; his furry head now had my lipstick mark. 'Oh, sorry – I'll wash it off tonight.' I left the house, giggling.

When I arrived at the restaurant, I was escorted to a table in a private booth. I walked past a few tables and noticed a man staring at me. I hoped nothing was wrong with my outfit.

When I got to the booth, Chris had arrived. But he was not alone.

'Sir, your guest is here,' the waiter said to Chris.

My jaw dropped and my mind went blank when I saw a beautiful woman sitting next to Chris. Nope, let me rephrase it – a beautiful woman *snuggling up* to Chris.

'Oh, you're here,' Chris said with a flicker of thrill and joy in his eyes. 'Come, I will introduce Danielle to you.'

God knows how much I wanted to run, but out of respect, I stayed put. More than that, I put out my hand like a businesswoman. 'Hi, Danielle, I am Anna Bell. Nice to meet you.'

'Hi, Anna.'

'Danielle is one of the faculty heads at the Design Institute,' Chris said with an admiring gaze. I didn't know why he admired her. In fact, I didn't care what feelings he had for her, I just wanted to go home. 'Her institute is going to make a reality TV show and is seeking a make-up artist as a judge.'

At this point, I kind of knew what was happening. Chris was selling me to a TV show, one that could increase my reputation and raise my salary. Yeah, that sounded great. But did it have to happen today?

'That sounds great...' I decided to play ball, well, it wasn't like I had any other choice, right? 'I should have brought my portfolio.' I laughed.

'Isn't your portfolio right here?' Danielle smiled and nodded her head to Chris. 'This is the perfect portfolio.'

'Trust me, I have a lot better than this.' I giggled.

'I don't need much of a makeover, you see.' Chris laughed, and his eyes sparkled with a seductive glimmer. 'I am already perfect.'

Danielle and I both rolled our eyes.

The rest of the dinner was fruitful, at least that was how it looked.

Before dessert, I visited the bathroom, just to take off my business mask for a while.

The fake laughing and meaningless conversations had worn me out. I'd already had a long working day, spent hours on styling for this dinner, and the worst part was I was now broke due to the expensive clothing. All I wanted now was to take a bath and hug Snowball to sleep.

I checked myself in the mirror; my outfit was perfect. I was damn sure I looked a thousand times better than Danielle, but Chris hadn't given me any appreciative glances; he just acted as if I was wearing my daily work outfit.

All that effort and all those expectations had gone down the drain.

I talked to myself in the mirror. 'What do you expect, Anna? Never a year, huh.' I gave myself a wry smile, felt ashamed and stupid.

After I'd let out my sadness, I put my mask back on to resume my 'business' dinner. When I got to the booth, what I saw shocked me as much as if I had witnessed a murder.

Danielle had leaned her head on Chris's shoulder, and her fingers were locked with Chris's. The worst part was that Chris showed no sign of pushing her away. I didn't know how long they had been in that position, but it was already too long for me.

When Chris saw me, he skilfully unlocked his fingers and moved away from Danielle.

'Hey, dessert is here.' He smiled.

When I returned to my seat, Danielle didn't even bother to look at me. She continued smiling seductively at Chris as if she was still intoxicated by the moment.

I couldn't watch any more of this vulgar scene. I needed to leave before I tore off my friendly mask.

'I'm sorry, but I need to leave. My dog is sick.' I grabbed my handbag.

'What's wrong with him?' Chris looked nervous.

'I guess he needs me,' I said. 'It's not a big deal, but I need to get home now. You two should stay.' I marched to the exit. 'Thanks for the dinner, by the way.'

When I got home, Snowball rushed over, giving me a warm welcome. I looked down to his head; the lipstick mark I'd left on his fur brought out the miserable memories of tonight. It triggered my emotions and I could no longer withhold my tears.

People said animals could feel emotions; well, now I could test that theory. Snowball leaned over and licked my face. I looked at his big round eyes and that smiley face – he was trying to comfort me. I hugged him in my arms, crying out all my anger and disappointment.

The girls get the hint and finally leave on their own. Derek's voice once again flashed in my head.

'Is this the hint?' I looked at Snowball, knowing that if I left I would forever be separated from him. But it seemed that it was not something I could control. In the end, I was the one who would be kicked out, right?

'Will you be fine without me?'

Snowball started whining at me. He put his paw on my lap as if he were stopping me from leaving.

'I love you, Snowball, but this is not my decision.' I softly petted his head, treasuring my last moment with him.

I looked around, trying to capture all the happy moments that had happened in this flat, because once I left, they would all forever be in my past.

Before Chris returned, I took a shower and jumped into bed. I didn't want to be confronted by him.

But that was silly; he never said anything when he returned, as if nothing had happened.

I guessed this was it; this was the hint.

CHAPTER EIGHT

'Make a wish, Anna,' the voice of my mum whispered in my ear.

The birds woke me with their squeaky song. I looked out of the window; the sky was grey and the street was empty, and the trees waved their yellowish leaves following the rhythm of the chilly wind.

It had been my first night in this newly rented house.

Quitting Chris also meant quitting my job and moving to a new place. I rented an Airbnb the day after I left the job. I needed a fresh start and to put things behind me. Fortunately, I found a new job at a music company called Magnum and a house to rent a week after I quit. Being jobless and homeless is not good for a single person.

My alarm rang, warning me not to be late for the first day of work. I got out of bed, put away my haunted face, and embraced my new job with a fake smile.

'Welcome on board, Anna.' My new manager, Karen, reached for a handshake. 'I hope my assistant has shown you around.' She looked at the young man behind me.

'Yes, the place is lovely.'

'Great. So let's discuss your role.' She sat down as she spoke, and politely gestured for me to sit next to her.

'I understand that you have worked as a Production Assistant before.'

I nodded and Karen continued. 'Great. I want to assign you to Jess Barner as her assistant and make-up artist, just temporarily.' She hesitated, perhaps knowing she had assigned me jobs that were outside my scope.

Being an assistant was not at the top of the list of things I wanted to do, but under the circumstances, I didn't have a choice. I nodded.

A smile rose on Karen's face. She then briefed me on the job details for the coming week.

Jess Barner was a young singer in her mid-twenties. She released her first album at the age of seventeen and it went straight into the top ten. She was a country music singer, but once in a while, she would do pop songs. My role was to assist her in all kinds of aspects, as well as be responsible for her make-up and styling. The company said this would be a great opportunity to learn new things, but this was just a fancy way to ask me to work extra hours.

After the briefing, the assistant brought me to Jess's changing room.

A soft and powdery scent of flowers filled my lungs when I entered the room. My gaze was caught by the large pile of lilies on the dressing table.

'They're beautiful,' I said out loud.

'Take them if you want,' a melodious voice said.

I looked for the owner of the voice and saw a woman on the other side of the room, lying on her back on the sofa, playing with her mobile. I was not a fan of hers, but the pink short hair was so significant that I knew instantly she was Jess Barner.

'You're my assistant?' she asked.

'Yes, also your make-up artist.'

'Multi-tasking, huh.' Jess smirked. 'This company is so stingy.'

I laughed.

'Nice to meet you by the way.' Jess jumped up to greet me.

'Nice to meet you too. I'm Anna Bell.'

'Anna, quick question. Cat or dog?'

'Huh?' I was surprised by her question.

'Do you like cats or dogs?'

'Um...' The image of Snowball came into my head, followed by his owner. I took a deep breath and wanted to shake away all the bad memories.

'Dogs,' I answered.

'Yeah!' Jess grabbed my hand. 'We can be friends.'

I looked at the gleam in her eyes, sparkling with excitement and happiness. Never had I encountered such rare innocence and open personality in this industry; her action astounded me.

'Yeah!' I placed my other hand over hers. 'So about today—'

'Oh, don't be boring, let's have some fun first.'

'Fun?'

The cold wind hit my face, and my hair flew back. I felt

breathless, I was going to faint, I didn't know how I'd ended up here today.

'Ah!' I heard screaming; it was Jess.

'This is so...!' she shouted, but the strong wind ate some of her words.

'I'm going to die.' I used my remaining breath to shout out my last words.

'No!' Jess shouted again. 'We're going to live!'

We got off the crazy roller coaster, and my legs were so weak that I almost fainted.

Jess put on her sunglasses and stood strong under the sun like a fighter.

'You are my assistant. You can do better than this.' Jess laughed.

'I'm too old for this.' I sat down nearby to calm my nerves.

'So are you better now?' Jess sat next to me, examining my face.

'Fine, just a bit dizzy,' I said.

Jess gave me a warm smile. 'Good.' She gently patted my shoulder like an old friend.

Perhaps I was imagining it, but there was a second when I thought it might not be my roller-coaster experience that she was referring to, but my miserable, haunted-looking face that she was concerned about. This was her way of cheering me up.

Jess looked at her watch and asked, 'Are we late? Don't we need to be at the studio now?'

I was too caught up in my thoughts and forgot I was actually working. 'Oh no!' I groaned.

We hopped into the car and quickly drove to our destination.

It was super fun working with Jess; she was humorous and cheerful, and her affection for people was so strong that even my negative personality was altered. I wouldn't say I was chirpy, but at least my dreadful memories had not surfaced since I'd worked with her. I tried never to think of it, or perhaps I had no time to, I was so busy with Jess. Apart from working with her, we hung out during our private time too. She loved to explore the city and we drove everywhere and tried different foods. It was like my miserable life never existed.

'Psst...'

I looked around and saw Jess standing next to the stage, indicating with her head. I followed her cue and saw a tall and muscular man on stage. He was wearing a black T-shirt and trousers and had a headset on. He must have been one of the production crew.

I mouthed the word 'What' to her.

Jess pointed her fingers together, mimicking two people kissing.

I quickly understood her intention, flung my arms akimbo and shot her a killing stare. When I was about to march toward her to strangle her, I saw a smile on her face, and she covered her mouth as she started giggling.

'Hi.'

I looked up to the stage; that production guy had spoken to me.

'Hi.' I smiled and tried to act normal. I could see from the corner of my eye that Jess was dancing like a cheerleader.

'I'm Nick, and you are...?'

'Anna.'

'Nice to meet you, Anna – you're Jess's assistant?'

I nodded.

'Do you need a walkie?' He passed me a walkie-talkie.

'I don't think I need it. I'll be around Jess all day.'

'Okay, I am the stage manager today, so if you need anything just ask me.' He shot me a smile. 'I'll be around here.'

I nodded and watched him walk to the other side of the stage.

Jess jumped next to my side. 'Did he ask you out?'

'He just asked if I need a walkie.' I rolled my eyes trying to calm my urge to kill this girl.

'Oh, he wants you to have *his* walkie.' Jess looked at me with her goofy eyes.

'Yeah, yeah, yeah.' I pushed Jess to her changing room. 'You better get ready.'

After the show, I sent Jess back to the changing room to prepare for the next job. She had handed me a mic from the show, so I went back to the stage to return it.

I walked toward Nick and he flashed a smile when saw me. 'Finished?'

'Yeah. Just come back to return this.' I passed him the mic.

As I went to turn around and return to the changing room, Nick stopped me.

'Anna.'

'Yes?' I paused. But he didn't say anything; he only stared at me with wide eyes.

'Oh no...' He flashed me a sheepish smile. 'I don't know what to say.'

I was confused.

'Sorry, I am usually very good at this...' He paused as if he'd suddenly realised a slip of the tongue. 'No, I don't mean flirting. I don't flirt ... I mean I am good with people, communicating with people.' His stuttering made him look cute.

I couldn't stop myself from giggling out loud.

'I just made a fool of myself, didn't I?' He looked down to the floor.

'No, you're fine.' I smiled. 'What can I help you with?'

He looked up with flushed cheeks. 'Just wondering if you would like to go to dinner? Becky Sushi?'

'Oh...' His sudden forward movement made me lose my mind. 'Um...'

My embarrassed reaction probably made him realise he had asked the wrong person.

'Oh, sorry,' he said. 'You have a boyfriend?'

I nodded reluctantly. Even though this was not true, it was the best step downward.

We quickly said goodbye and I left.

The next day when we were in a studio changing room, out of nowhere, Jess asked a super-personal question. 'Are you gay?'

Her sudden question almost made me choke. 'No.' I laughed. 'Why do you think I am?'

'Then why won't you go out with Nick?'

'Who's Nick?' I asked.

Jess cackled out loud. 'Oh, come on – Nick, the stage manager from yesterday?'

I flipped through my memory, and an image of a tall, muscular guy faintly rose.

'Why would I go out with him? Besides...' I thought about my conversation with Nick. 'He never asked me out.'

'He asked you to go Becky Sushi with him, remember?'

'But I hate sushi.'

Jess rolled her eyes and looked as if she was going to explode. 'Then you can suggest other places.'

'But I don't want to suggest other places, I don't want to go out with him.'

'Why not?'

'Why yes?'

'Have you seen his body?' Jess groaned.

It was my turn to roll my eyes. 'You can find those types of guys in any gym.' I smirked at Jess. 'Come on, you're my boss, you can do better than this.'

Jess burst into laughter. 'Fine, challenge accepted. I, Jess Barner, will find you a gorgeous man that you cannot resist.'

I smiled and walked out of the room. But as soon as I stepped out the door, my cheerful feelings froze.

It was not hard to figure out that the stage manager liked me; it was just that I was not ready to meet anyone yet, at least not now. The thought of losing someone important again would eat me alive. I was not sure if I dared to do it again.

Recordings, live shows, interviews, modelling ... it had been a crazy week. Jess and I had been all over the country, working non-stop.

'I need a break,' Jess said. 'I slept like three hours a day for the whole week. This is unbearable.'

I supported her with a yawn. 'Tell me about it.'

We walked to her personal changing room, preparing to end the day.

As I opened the door, the scent of lilies emerged and woke a memory.

'Lilies again, huh.' I pointed to the pile of lilies on the dressing table.

Instead of flashing a 'happily in love' expression, Jess just coldly glanced at the flowers and walked past them. She lay back on the sofa and closed her eyes to rest.

'So...' I walked over to the sofa, lifted her legs and sat next to her. 'Who sent you those flowers?' I smirked.

'Nobody,' Jess said with her eyes shut.

'Come on, I can keep a secret.'

'You can keep the flowers.'

'Fine.'

Her silence was a cue for me to mind my own business. Having been working with Jess for over half a year, I knew my position.

'Okay, I will give you some peace,' I said as I stood up from the sofa.

I took my backpack and was about to open the door.

'He's married,' Jess said in a cold, distant voice.

Her words came like a bombshell; my hand paused on the doorknob, and my feet were stapled on the floor.

'What?' I raised my voice.

Jess was already sitting up on the sofa, looking at me with a sadness in her eyes that I seldom saw.

'I didn't know until I was too far in.'

Well, at least Chris wasn't married or lying to me. One point to Anna in the lucky life competition.

'You've broken up with him then?' I said.

'What else could I do?'

'Was the break-up bad?'

'Well, if crying and snapping is bad, then yes, it was pretty bad.'

'Shame,' I said.

'What do you mean?' She frowned.

'You should have got him to buy you an expensive dinner, then broken up with him.'

Jess burst out laughing. 'Yes, I should have made him buy me a three-Michelin-star dinner.'

'Was he good-looking?'

My questions dropped her mood slightly, and she gave me a sheepish smile. 'Yes, quite fit.'

'Damn, Jess, you should have had him five times the night before breaking up with him.'

Jess once again burst into laughter. 'Anna!' She pretended to be angry, but the smile on her face didn't scare me.

'He's bad in bed?' I said, acting innocent, my eyes wide.

'I swear, Anna, if you say one more thing about sex, I will kick your ass.' The cute angry face on Jess was so funny.

'Fine.' I opened the door and was about to step out. 'Was he well-endowed?'

When I saw Anna take the pillow in her hand, I smoothly walked out of the room.

'Anna!' she shouted as she threw the pillow behind me.

Another busy week for us.

'What would you do if you weren't a make-up artist?' Jess asked as we got in the car. She was too tired to drive today, so had her driver take us back home.

'Don't know, probably a librarian.'

'You like to read?' Jess frowned, looking sceptical.

'No.' I chuckled. 'Just thought I would look hot as a librarian.'

Jess laughed. 'You can still look hot in other jobs.'

'No, librarians look geeky hot, not as much as a scientist but not dumpy either. Kind of in the middle, not too intimidating.'

Jess shook her head and laughed. 'I want to be a housewife...' Her voice trailed off. I guessed her bad memories intruded again. 'Don't you ever dream of marrying someone you love?'

Her question made me snort with laughter. *Dream? I don't even dare to think.* Any thought of Chris would probably lead to another weeping and sobbing episode that I didn't want.

'Hey...' Jess sent a punch to my shoulder. 'Don't laugh at people's dreams.'

I ignored her words. 'So you are ready to give up your achievement – being in the top ten on Spotify – for a man?'

She thought long and deeply. 'Fine.' She leaned back in her seat. 'That I want it doesn't necessarily mean I'm going out to get it.'

'Then there's no point in this conversation.' I smirked.

'But...'

I saw the screen on my vibrating phone. 'Shush! It's Karen,' I cried.

Jess zipped her mouth, but quietly landed a punch on my arm.

'Are you coming back to the office today?' Karen asked.

'No, but I could if you need me.' I only said it out of courtesy, and I hoped she would ask me not to bother.

'Yes, would that be okay for you?'

Damn, I planned to go home and watch Netflix.

'Sure. I'll come to the office now.'

I got out of the car and grabbed an Uber to the office. By the time I arrived, it was almost 6.30 p.m.

The receptionist had left and the office was half empty. I went to Karen's office and realised she was still in a meeting, so I went to the kitchen to get myself some juice.

The fridge contained all sorts of cold pressed juice: apple, pineapple, orange, and kiwi. They all looked amazing and tasty.

'Excuse me.' A man spoke from behind the fridge door.

I leaned back. It was a beautiful young man.

Yes, beautiful.

'Can I help you?' I asked.

'Do you know if Jo Swindon from HR is still at the office?' His voice was soft and gentle.

'No, sorry.'

'It's okay, thanks.'

He took off quickly.

I looked at the clock; it was almost 7 p.m. I went to Karen's office again and was glad to see her alone this time.

'Hi.' I knocked on the door as I spoke. 'You need me?'

Karen looked up from behind a pile of documents and hard folders. When her eyes fell on me, she smiled. 'Anna, hi!' she said. 'Please, take a seat.' She motioned to a chair as she spoke. 'So how have you been?'

'Fine.'

'I've heard that you worked well with Jess.'

'Yes, she's very nice and great to work with.'

'I'm glad to hear it.' She seemed to hesitate. 'Anna...'

'Yes?' Her conspiratorial look made me nervous.

Fear of being fired sped up my heartbeat.

'Would you like a new challenge?'

I will jump over a fire for you, just don't fire me.

'Sure,' I said.

Karen took a breath of relief. 'That's great. Thank you, Anna.'

After a minute of silence, I became impatient. 'May I know what the task is?'

'Oh yes.' Karen smiled, realising she had forgotten to brief me. 'I would like to reassign you to another person.' She looked down at her document.

'But what about—'

'She will be fine,' Karen said without looking up. 'I will assign another assistant for Jess.'

'Okay. So who will that—'

A knock on the door attracted our attention, and my eyes fell on a beautiful man at the door. It was the man from the kitchen.

'Let me introduce you to Ryan Norton,' Karen said and gestured for Ryan to come in. 'Ryan, I want you to meet your new assistant and make-up artist, Anna Bell.'

★ ★ ★ ★

As soon as I got home, my phone rang. I was not surprised to see it was Jess calling.

'Oh no, Anna,' Jess groaned on the other end of the phone. 'How can she do that?'

I threw my bag onto the sofa and fell on top of it. 'Well, she kind of can. She is our manager, remember?' I chuckled.

'How can you be cool about that?' she roared.

'What can I do? If I refuse her request, who is going to pay my rent?'

Jess mumbled something about not being fair, feeling disappointed.

'Come on, sweetie, I'm just working with other people, not going to Mars. We can still meet,' I said, but another part of me felt sweet and warm. I was glad she treated me so well, and I'd never had such a close friend before. It was kind of new and exciting for me.

'Fine, but you promise to meet me whenever you're free?' she said. I could imagine her pulling her face like a grumpy old woman.

'Promise.'

'So when will the change be?'

'About that…' It was really hard to tell her the truth. 'Tomorrow.'

'What?' Jess's voice was so loud that I had to pull the phone away from my ear.

'Yeah, I'm sorry.'

After that, I spent thirty minutes trying to calm her down and assure her that everything would be fine.

But would it truly be fine?

CHAPTER NINE

Ryan Norton had joined the industry two years ago. I was assigned to him as stylist and temp assistant.

'So...' Ryan glanced at me before he continued. 'Maybe we can introduce ourselves?' He opened the car door for me.

My first job with him was to visit a radio station. After a simple makeover in the changing room, we headed out to the car park. Ryan drove his own vehicle and invited me to join him. I had to accept his offer because there was no transportation allowance, even though I wasn't too happy.

I liked the idea of the free ride, but I was scared to be trapped in the same space with another guy.

'Do you want to go first?' Ryan asked after I gave him zero response.

'Um, sure,' I answered reluctantly. 'I'm Anna Bell,' I said as I glanced at him.

He was watching me and looked amused.

'What's wrong?' I asked.

His gorgeous blue eyes widened as he gave me a big smile. 'That's it?' He laughed. 'Just Anna Bell?'

I was confused. 'Well, I've worked here for over half a year.'

He cackled with laughter but looked away this time. He turned to the wheel and started the engine. 'This is not a job interview, Anna.' He shot me a glance before putting all his focus behind the wheel.

After that, he never spoke a word, and I began to wonder if he was angry with my cold attitude. But I had to put that behind me because my phone rang; it was an interview request from a reporter. When the call was finished, more came. By the time I had answered over ten calls and messages, we had arrived at the radio station.

DJ Joey greeted us in the recording room. 'Right on time!'

'As always.' Ryan hugged him like they were old friends.

'You've got a new assistant!' Joey said when he saw me standing behind Ryan.

After a brief exchange, they went to the room behind the glass wall and began the programme.

Now I had time to take a closer look at Ryan.

He had medium-length blond hair and blue eyes, a teenage boyish style, and was of medium build. Whenever he smiled, it felt like the sun shone through my soul. If Chris was the devil, Ryan would be an angel. They were different types, yet both were extremely attractive.

After the interview, we had about two hours of spare time before the next job.

Ryan suggested that we grab lunch together. I was too hungry to refuse his invitation and I let him pick the location. But I regretted it the minute our car stopped in front of a busy Italian restaurant.

'You must be kidding,' I said.

'What do you mean?' Ryan looked puzzled.

'Have you seen how many people are in there?' I asked. 'Or do you want to eat in the car?'

Ryan relaxed and smiled. 'It's fine. Come with me.'

I followed him in full-on alert mode, thinking about what to do if we were seen by his fans. Instead of walking in through a side door, he used the front door like the general public.

What?

As we entered the restaurant, a beautiful blonde walked over and hugged Ryan. The woman was in her fifties but still looked amazingly hot.

Ryan smiled like a sun. 'This is my colleague, Anna.' He patted my shoulder like we were friends. 'Anna, this is my aunt Christine. She has taken care of me for a long time.'

'Yep, I know every one of his dark secrets.' Christine smiled and gave me a wink.

'Whoo, I know who to find when someone doesn't behave!' I laughed.

Ryan rolled his eyes while Christine chuckled. She led us to a booth near a window at the back, and after she put down some semi-sheer curtains, we had the space to ourselves, private and comfy.

'My aunt owns this place,' Ryan said after we ordered.

'Really? That's loads of work.' I was surprised because it wasn't a small restaurant; there were around thirty staff at the front and probably twenty or more in the kitchen.

'Yes, the restaurant was her husband's, Dave. But after he passed away, it passed on to her.' The temperature dropped as he spoke, and those sunshine smiles on his face vanished leaving the air cold and stuffy.

'I'm sorry to hear that,' I said. 'Were you close to your uncle?'

I could never imagine a person could be described as a storm, but now that storm appeared in front of me.

Sadness overtook him as if he was going to burst into tears. When I thought he was going to cry, he lifted the corners of his lips, sharing the most miserable smile I had ever seen.

'I don't remember because he passed away when I was young.' He glanced at me and continued. 'He was in a car crash with my parents. They all died on the scene.'

Soft and juicy, the chicken should have tasted amazing, yet it felt like eating tasteless cardboard. The spaghetti was chewy and soft, like authentic Italian, but it felt like shoelaces in my mouth.

People say your mood affects your taste buds. I never believed that until now.

Before the food arrived, Ryan told me his tragic story, a story that was so similar to mine; for a second, I wondered if he was playing a prank on me.

'I don't recall much, but I still remember the sound of the raindrops splashing on the window when my aunt came over and whispered to me "Everything will be fine".'

Even though the restaurant was crowded and warm and filled with noisy customers, there was a cold silence between us.

I tried to speak, say something comforting, but nothing came out of my mouth.

I glanced at him and he returned the gaze, neither of us willing to look away until the waitress had served us the meal. I tried hard to finish what was on the plate. I knew the food was delicious, but his story had disconnected my taste buds and turned my meal into tasteless cardboard.

My mood had dramatically dropped, and the memory I was unwilling to recall was waving at me from the corner. Tears were making their way out.

I took a deep breath, trying to breathe out all the depression that was trapped in my body.

'Are you feeling all right?' Ryan said. 'Looked as if you were the one telling the story.' He chuckled.

I looked down at my fingers and tried to smile because no matter how much I wanted to deny it, the truth was we shared the same tragic story. But I planned to keep that in the dark.

'It's fine, it happened a long time ago,' he continued. 'I have overcome the past.' He peeked outside the booth. 'Besides, I still have my auntie. She's taken great care of me all these years.' He smiled.

I was not sure if I had just paid a visit to heaven, but I swore I saw an angel sitting opposite me. Ryan shot me the most innocent smile I have ever seen on a human being. The sadness that had built inside me collapsed into dust and was burned away by that sunny smile.

I opened my mouth but hesitated.

Our past was like a reflection in a mirror, and if I shared my story, we would probably burst into tears and start to lick each other's wounds. But that wasn't what I wanted; the only thing I needed then was distance.

'Do you tell your story to everyone you just met?' I chuckled.

I wasn't trying to be rude, but I needed to find a way to end this conversation.

'Not really.' He smiled and cast me a playful glance. 'Not everyone. Why do you ask?'

'Just a tiny suggestion.' I leaned my arm on the table and cupped my face in my palm. 'You might want to revise your introduction to something more positive,' I said with a yawn. 'It's too depressing.'

It might have been my words, or possibly my yawn that froze Ryan, but the shock didn't last long, and he burst into laughter after a few seconds of silence.

'Why are you laughing?' I put on a puzzled face, acting dumb. But behind this poker face, I was secretly relieved that he'd lightened the mood.

'I admire the way you comfort people.' He chuckled. 'Fine, I will scrap the whole sad story thing, but you'll need to help me think of a good alternative since you're the one who suggested it.'

'Fair enough. Let me ask something about you then.' I sipped my tea and took my time to think of questions.

I asked, 'How old are you?'

'Twenty-five,' he answered. 'And you?'

I guess I need to reply.

'I'm twenty-eight. Zodiac sign?'

'Pisces. And you?'

'Cancer. Do you have a pet?'

'None, and you?'

'Nope. Have a house?'

'Not yet. And you?'

'Nope. Have a girlfriend?'

'Nope, and you?'

'What kind of sport do you like?'

'Running...' Ryan suddenly paused. 'Hey!' He held up his hands with his palms facing up. 'You skipped my question.'

I chuckled. 'Remember, I'm the one asking questions.'

'I don't care, do you have a boyfriend?'

I hesitated for three seconds. 'Nope.'

'Why the hesitation?'

'I didn't.' I laughed.

'Sounds suspicious!' Ryan squinted his eyes. His baby face made me giggle loudly.

'My boyfriend is this job.' I laughed. 'I'm married to this job.'

'What a coincidence!' Ryan laughed. 'Me too! We can go on a double date!'

Both of us burst into laughter.

'I can see you love your job a lot!' I said.

'Well, yes.' Ryan calmed himself. 'But I needed to overcome a lot of issues to do this.' He sent me a wry smile.

'What issues? Too handsome?' I teased.

He burst into laughter again.

'No!' He giggled. 'Besides, I'm not that handsome.'

'Yeah, and a millionaire is not rich.'

My words again made him giggle like a little boy.

'So what's the real reason then?' I asked after he calmed himself.

'My aunt didn't want me to.' He peeked into the restaurant, looking at his aunt who was behind the cash desk. 'She wanted me to finish university.'

'That makes sense. Still, you ended up here with me.' I laughed. 'What went wrong?'

'Modelling.' He scratched his head and looked as if he was a little boy who got caught drawing on the wall. 'I wanted to make some money for my aunt, so I started modelling secretly for a magazine.'

'Is that a magazine for aliens?' I giggled. 'It wouldn't be a secret when your photo was published, right?'

'Yeah.' He looked down at the table with flushed cheeks. His embarrassment made me feel bad for teasing him, but the innocent action was hilarious. 'My aunt saw my photo in a magazine and she was furious.'

'Of course she was.'

'But in just one day of shooting, I earned more than half a month's salary at a supermarket.'

'Do you need that money though? I mean your aunt does own a restaurant – you're not actually in financial difficulties.'

'No, but I didn't want to be a spoilt kid who would just spend money. I wanted to earn it too.' He took a sip of water. 'Anyway, after I had been modelling for a year, I was approached by Magnum. They invited me for an audition. I went to the audition, sang a song, and here I am.'

'With millions of fans.' I scoffed. 'You make it sound so easy.'

'Well, indeed, joining the industry was not that difficult for me, but my aunt...' He flashed another wry smile. 'She was enraged – she went to the company and questioned our manager.'

'Karen? She confronted Karen?' My eyes widened and I leaned forward. I was in thrall. 'Did it get physical?'

'What? No.' Ryan laughed. 'She asked Karen to cancel the contract. But Karen asked her to calm down and brought her to the recording room.'

'For what?'

'To let her listen to my recording.' Ryan flashed me a sheepish smile. 'After that, she agreed to let me join the company.'

'You must have an angelic voice.'

'I don't think so ... but you've never listened to my music?' Ryan looked disappointed.

'Well...' I suddenly felt unprofessional because I'd never listened to the work of my work partner. 'I will listen to it tonight.'

Ryan pouted like a little child, and his sweet face gave me the urge to pet his hair.

'It's fine,' he said with a smile, but he still looked disappointed. 'How about you?'

'Me?'

'How did you end up here with me?'

This was a simple question, yet it created a pain that travelled through my body like thousands of needles in my flesh. The olive eyes flashed through my mind; my stomach twitched and my heart pounded. After all this time, I still had a strong affection for him.

'Are you okay?' Ryan looked at me with a concerned gaze. 'You look pale.'

'I'm fine.' I smiled, flushing all the terrible past into my gut. 'Well, I wanted to look pretty, so I joined the industry.'

I took a sip of water and then quietly looked at Ryan.

After a moment of silence, he burst into laughter.

'Oh, come on.' He laughed. 'That's it? I told you my whole story and you give me eight words?'

'Ten to be exact.' I giggled.

'No, no, no, Anna, I need more.' He leaned forward and placed his hands on the table. 'We are not leaving until you tell me something about you in more than a hundred words.'

He stared at me in silence while I giggled like a child. Watching his serious face, I understood I would not get away with it today.

I slowly leaned forward like him and rested my arm on the table. In my head, I put my story in sequence and, when I was ready, I started telling my story – well, part of my story.

'When I was young, I wasn't a confident person. I always felt a need to motivate my mind and change my life, I didn't want to be trapped in a dull world, so I thought it would be cool to do something in the fashion industry. You know, *glamour and luxury*.'

'Why not be a model or designer then?' Ryan questioned.

'Well, I'm not pretty enough to be a model and not talented enough to be a designer, that's why.'

'Don't sell yourself short.'

'I'm not undervaluing myself,' I argued, 'I'm just being practical. Besides, I like make-up and styling. Every time I lift my brush, I feel like a wizard casting a spell. Not only could I beautify people's appearance, but I could see their confidence build dramatically.'

'Really?' He looked intrigued. 'I never understand why people need to cover their face with make-up.'

'Beautiful people like you will never understand.' I rolled my eyes.

'Looks don't really matter,' he said genuinely. 'It's the heart.'

'And money doesn't matter.' I rolled my eyes. 'Said the billionaire.'

'Oh, please – we will all grow old one day and lose our beauty. The heart will stay beautiful forever.' Ryan looked straight into my eyes, into my soul. 'Besides, I think you're beautiful enough without make-up.'

His sudden praise of me warmed my heart and heated my face.

'You don't think so?' Ryan chuckled.

'I think it's time for us to leave.' I got up.

'No way.' He grabbed my arm and pulled me back onto the chair. 'You haven't finished your story.'

I sighed. 'Where were we again?'

'You started learning make-up and styling.'

'Yeah, so normal people–' I pointed to myself '–want to look good to build up their confidence, so I decided to learn make-up and styling. I was lucky enough to do it professionally to earn a living. After a year of working freelance, one day, I started working for Marie McKey—'

'You've worked for Marie McKey?' Ryan widened his blue eyes, making them look huge. 'The fashion icon Marie McKey?'

'Yes, she was the one who brought me into this industry. With her introduction, I've had the chance to work with lots of big-name celebrities.'

'Such as…?'

'Katie Queen, Lisa M, Jo Brad—'

'Wow, Lisa M?'

I nodded.

'Any more famous people? Any men?'

His questions once again stuck needles in my flesh; the pain was like a reminder of caution. Be aware of what you are going to say.

'Nelson Smith, John Charles.'

'That's it?' Ryan raised his eyebrows, looking in disbelief.

I nodded but was unable to lock eyes with him. I looked at the clock on the wall.

'Oh no!' I yelled. 'We're going to be late.'

Ryan took a look at his watch and stood up immediately. 'It's your fault for talking so much.'

I raised my eyebrows. 'What?' I howled. 'You are—'

'Oh, you need to learn when to stop talking.' He chuckled.

'Ryan Norton!'

⭐ ⭐ ⭐

'All the fans are gathered here, just to see one person...' The anchor stood in front of a group of fans. Spotlights and cameras were all pointed at her.

The fans behind were mostly teenage girls; they were so excited and held signs that said 'Ryan'. To prevent chaos, they had to stand behind crowd-control barriers that separated them from the reporter's area.

When the cameraman gave a signal to the crew, they sent Ryan to the reporter. As he entered the spotlight, all the fans screamed like crazy. They were too enthusiastic; some tried to climb over the barrier but were stopped by the security men. Ryan turned around and waved to them, which made the crowd even more excited. I hadn't seen such a crazy situation for so long; I was used to working with more mature celebrities and their fans were a bit older and calmer.

'How are you, Ryan?'

'Hello, Phoebe, I'm great.'

'Your fans are so enthusiastic.'

'Yes, they are.' Ryan smiled.

I looked at this young celebrity, admiring his perfect features. Ryan was quite tall and medium built. His face was symmetrical and every angle was photograph-ready. Under those spotlights, his shoulder-length blond hair was like gold thread; his skin was soft like marshmallow and when he smiled, it felt like the sunshine on your soul. I understood why those fans were so deeply in love with this angel boy.

After the interview, we got in the car heading to the studio for a photo shoot. Ryan looked a bit tired. I carefully checked his face to plan what cosmetics to use later.

'You seem a bit tired,' I said. 'Are you okay?'

He leaned his head on the seat back and turned his face to me. 'Maybe.' He wore a tired smile.

'This is our last job for today, can you make it?' I checked the calendar on my phone.

'Can I say no?'

'You cannot.' I grinned.

He snorted.

I tried to cheer him up. 'Come on, happy Friday!'

'It's not happy if I have nowhere to go tonight.'

'Isn't home a happy place to be?'

'Not if there's no one there.'

'Your aunt?'

'I don't live with my aunt.'

'Well, then buy a pizza and go home to watch TV.'

'Netflix and chill?'

'You can do that.' I laughed.

'Nah.'

He shot me a sparkling gaze. 'Anna...' he said and lifted a sunny smile.

For the first time, my heart sped up just from seeing his signature sunny smile. However, that angel's smile felt a bit sneaky.

'What are you doing tonight?' he asked. 'How about...'

'No.' I immediately knew what he was planning.

'You haven't even heard what I was going to say.' Ryan raised his voice.

'I don't need to.'

'But are you going anywhere tonight?'

'No, but I'm not inviting you to my house.'

'Why not? I can buy the pizza,' he begged.

'I can buy my own pizza.'

'Isn't it better to share a pizza?'

'Did I not mention I am a selfish pig?'

After arguing throughout the journey to the studio, Ryan's energy seemed to have recharged.

'I see you are ready for the photo shoot.' I smiled.

'No.' Ryan's face turned sad and tired again. 'I still don't feel too well.'

I rolled my eyes and pushed him into the changing room. 'If you behave well, maybe...'

Before I finished the sentence, Ryan looked at me with sparkling eyes. 'I could visit your place!' His angel face was like a little child's and I hated to refuse any of his requests.

'We will see,' I answered.

Just like a kid who knew he would be rewarded, he was in an extremely efficient mood. He calmly sat still for my styling and listened carefully to all the instructions; it was hard not to give him a hundred points for today's behaviour.

I ordered two pizzas at a local restaurant. 'A large margarita and a large pepperoni.'

'Any drinks?'

'What do you have?'

'Soda, wine, beer.'

I wanted to order wine but hesitated as it seemed inappropriate.

'Two sodas, thanks.'

Ryan sat in his car waiting for me. I brought our food to the car and he quickly drove us back to my place.

My flat was far away from the penthouse I used to live in, for obvious reasons.

But I liked the modern decoration in my old home, so when I was searching for a place to live I looked for flats with a modern style.

It was not a big place – a one-bedroom flat in London Zone Three. It had a light grey open kitchen and a modern black and white bathroom. The bedroom was decorated in navy blue paint; the soothing colour easily calmed my emotions whenever I came back from work.

'You have good taste.' Ryan looked at the industrial-style wall in my sitting room, admiring the raw design. 'I like that.' He pointed at a painting of a Samoyed.

It was not Snowball, just a picture I bought online that resembled him. All this time, I could not forget about him and his master.

'I just randomly bought it online,' I said.

'Really?'

'Yeah, why?'

Ryan shook his head. 'Never mind,' he said as he lay on the sofa.

'What do you want to watch?' I switched on the television and looked for the TV schedule.

'Don't have a preference.'

When I got to the movie category and saw all the movie thumbnails, my instinct quickly warned me to abort.

I flipped through the options and it wasn't long before I

saw one of Chris's movies. I pretended I had no interest in any of them, and quickly turned to the TV pages.

'We're watching a TV show?' Ryan asked.

'Nothing interesting in the film section.' I glued my gaze to the TV.

'Oh...'

'Do you like detective shows?' I opened the *Sherlock Holmes* TV series thumbnail and studied the description.

Ryan didn't reply.

I took it as a no, so I skipped to the next one.

'Action?' I opened the *24* thumbnail, but again no feedback from Ryan.

'Romance?' I opened the *Love and Go* thumbnail, but he remained silent. So I turned around to check whether he had fallen asleep but instead I saw Ryan staring at me.

'What?' I asked.

He flashed a smile after he bit back what he was about to say.

I watched his hesitation, wondering if I had overlooked a genre. Well, there was always one type of show that guys liked a lot.

'Erotic?' I asked with wide eyes. 'I don't have tissues here – you need to watch that at your own home.'

'What? No!' He burst into laughter. 'And what's the tissue for?'

'I don't know, you boys,' I said. 'If it's not porn, then why can't you tell me what you want to watch?'

He slowly calmed down. 'How about *Friends*,' he said.

'You've never watched *Friends*?' I almost squealed. I couldn't believe anyone had not watched this classic comedy.

'Just play it, the pizza's getting cold,' Ryan said.

As the programme began, we each took a slice of pizza and leaned back to enjoy the food and the show.

I had watched this hundreds of times, especially in the months after I left Chris. The laughter in the background could soothe my sadness and bring life to the house. The jokes in the show sailed through my sadness and helped me to keep my feet on the ground.

Ryan suddenly spoke. 'This brings back a lot of memories. I remember this helped me to sail through most of my sad moments. The background sound is amazing.' He laughed.

'Yes...' I glued my gaze to the TV and lifted a wry smile. 'The laughing sound is very soothing.'

Neither of us spoke a word after that but just quietly watched the show. I wasn't really paying attention to any of the content, though, because memories of Chris flooded my mind.

※ ※ ※ ※

'Anna!'

I turned around and saw a beautiful woman wearing a white T-shirt and a pair of blue jeans with white sneakers. Time had left marks on her face, but ageing did not affect her beauty; she still looked stunning.

'Christine.' I was surprised to see Ryan's aunt in the mall on Sunday because I knew she needed to take care of her restaurant twenty-four seven.

'Surprised to see me here today?' Christine smiled. 'I don't work twenty-four seven. Sometimes I do take a break,' she said.

'I didn't know you were a psychic too.'

She burst into laughter.

'Well, there is a wedding going on in my restaurant, the chef is taking care of the whole thing. I wasn't needed anyway,' she said with a yawn. 'So what are you doing here?' she asked.

'I'm just stocking up materials for work.' I held up my shopping bag to show her. 'Cosmetics.'

'It must be wonderful to work while doing shopping,' she said. 'So have you finished your shopping for today?'

'Yes.'

'Would you like to join me for tea?'

'Oh.' I felt slightly uncomfortable because she was my colleague's family. I did not want to get too close to them *again*. 'Well, I was planning—'

'You know there's a new café down the mall and they serve amazing Japanese soufflé pancakes.' Christine's eyes sparkled with excitement.

The word pancakes caught my attention. 'Soufflé pancakes? What's that?'

'Apparently it's a fluffy pancake from Japan. It's soft with a mixture of egg and cream.' She pulled out her phone to show me images of the mysterious dessert.

The three-inch-high pancake decorated with whipped cream and strawberries kicked away my sensible mind. I would have done anything to get that fluffy thing into my mouth.

'Oh my!' I screamed with excitement. 'I need to try this.'

'Let's go then.' Christine wrapped her arm around me. 'It's on the ground floor.'

Before I made any response, Christine had already pulled me towards the elevator.

Oh well, one meal won't hurt.

When we got to the café, I was shocked to see the length of the queue.

'It will be hours before we can get in.' I raised my concern because I didn't want to spend my precious free time queuing, but then I was also dying to try out the pancakes.

'No worries.' Christine shot me a sunshine smile, one that reminded me of her angelic nephew.

She pulled me towards the café and when we got to the front of the queue, she left me and went to the waitress at the counter.

After a few seconds, she waved and gestured for me to enter.

We followed the waitress and were assigned a table next to the window.

'Let us know when you are ready to order.' The waitress gave us a menu and went to serve other customers.

'How did you get in without queuing?' I asked after the waitress left.

Christine looked around and shot me a smile. 'I know the owner of this place – he is a friend.'

'Wow, that's amazing.'

'I go to lots of food trade events to meet people from the industry.'

'It must be fun to meet all these interesting people.'

'Trust me, they're boring as hell.' She snorted. Then she looked at the queue outside the restaurant and said, 'But this is one of the good things to make up for it.' She pointed to the long queue outside.

The waiter soon returned to take our order.

Christine chose the chocolate soufflé pancake, and I ordered the signature strawberry soufflé pancake.

'How's work?' Christine asked after the waiter left.

'It's fine, quite busy lately though. Ryan's workloads are huge and wherever he goes, I follow.'

'You seem to be handling it quite well.'

'Well, I'm used to it,' I answered.

'You worked there for long?'

'Not really, I just joined this company less than a year ago, but I've been in the industry for over a decade. I've worked as a make-up artist ever since I finished college.'

'Wow, that's impressive. You must love this job so much.'

'Yes, this job is my life.'

'Sweetie, you are too beautiful to be married to your job.'

'I'm not anywhere near beautiful.' I laughed in embarrassment. 'I'm just too good at my job.' I shamelessly pointed at my face, showing her the make-up I wore today. 'Besides, I prefer working.'

'That's nonsense,' Christine said. 'We all need love and a person to lean on.'

A flash of memory reappeared. The image of Chris rose inside my head without my consent. Those olive-green eyes once again dragged me into a dark hole, destroying my weekend mood.

'Anna?' Christine shot me a concerned gaze. I guess my silence made her worried. 'Are you okay?'

I nodded, yet I knew I would not be okay for the rest of the day.

'Sorry for keeping you waiting. Here are your pancakes.' The waiter came just in time, giving time for me to rebuild my mood.

'Let's give it a try.' Christine didn't wait until the waiter left and put a piece of pancake into her mouth.

'Oh my...' She looked pleasantly surprised, and the

glimmer in her eyes silently put a thumbs-up to the pancake. I was intrigued by her expression and could not wait to join her in pancake paradise.

I put a piece into my mouth, and it did not take long for me to experience her surprise journey.

'It is soft like ... air.' It took me a while to figure out a word to describe this fluffy gourmet food. 'The creamy texture pairs well with the light whipped cream. I love that it is not overly sweet.'

'You have sensitive taste buds,' Christine said.

'Well, I don't know about that, but I love all kinds of food.' I laughed as I put another piece of pancake into my mouth. 'My second husband is probably food.'

Christine chuckled. 'Husbands are job and food! Anna, you can do better than that.'

'Well, that's the best I could do.' I laugh.

'Not interested in dating?' she asked.

'Not really.' Under her concerned gaze, I shut down my memories of Chris and tried to act calm and careless. 'I am too busy.'

Christine nodded but didn't say any further.

The short silence between us gave me a chance to breathe and put the depression behind me. But as time passed, I started to wonder if she was deliberately keeping quiet or if she'd run out of topics. I hoped it was the former because I am not good at starting small talk.

Fortunately, she broke the silence and my anxiety quickly disappeared. 'So what do you do in your leisure time?'

Why is everyone so concerned about my leisure time?

'I don't have many hobbies, but I sometimes use my free time to do part-time tutoring.'

'Like a make-up course?'

'Yes.'

'That's amazing!' Christine said with an envious gaze. 'I always wanted to start a cooking class. In fact, I was going to start one...' She let out a breath and slowly looked out of the window, her voice sounding distant. It was easy to tell that her mind had travelled to her past. 'But my husband passed away and I had to look after Ryan.' She shot me a mournful smile.

I looked at her and was lost for words.

'Did Ryan tell you his story?' she asked.

I nodded, not brave enough to move my lips to say anything further. Depression once again hit me like a car crash. It kept coming back whenever I'd almost got out of it. I could feel my stomach twist; tears were in the corner of my eyes, waiting for a keyword or signal to run down my cheek.

'I cannot believe it was over ten years ago.' Christine put another piece of pancake into her mouth. 'Sometimes, I forget they ever existed.' She smiled.

I looked down at my fork, too scared to hold my gaze on her, or was I fighting too hard to keep the tears in my eyes? Those seven words were like a feather, softly touching my soul.

'You know,' she continued without waiting for my response. 'Ryan shut himself down after that accident. It took quite a while for him to open up.'

'He's lucky that he has you.' I finally found my voice.

I looked up and was welcomed by a caring gaze; the smile on her was like the sun, wrapping my whole body and warming up my cold soul.

'No, we have each other,' she said. 'He is the reason I

needed to hold it together. He gave me the courage to step out from the past and bravely start a new chapter of life.'

I nodded, knowing anything I said would sound sour and bitter. Because unlike them, I had no one.

'Anna.' Christine leaned forward and gently grabbed my hand. 'I am not an expert but if you need someone to talk to, you can always come and find me.' She squeezed my hand to reinforce her words. 'You don't have to fight this all alone.'

'How...' My trembling voice shocked me. I calmed myself and cleared my throat 'How do you know?'

'You're just like Ryan after the accident.'

A sharp clinking sound rose in my head as if unlocking a chain to open Pandora's box. My tears slowly dropped like rainfall. I had let go of myself, given up on holding on to the sadness that grew inside me.

'I'm sorry,' I said with a smile. 'I...' Further denial was useless when trying to stop the tears, but I didn't want to admit the resemblance of my past with his. I didn't want to admit my loved ones were gone and the fact that, sometimes, I also forgot they had ever existed.

Christine moved her chair closer to me and hugged me into her shoulder. Her warm gesture slowly melted my guard. After all these years, every lonely night vanished. For once, I had found a shoulder to lean on.

★ ★ ★ ★

It was eight o'clock when I returned home.

The incident today had me crying like a baby, yet I was glad it had happened.

Christine was like a psychologist patiently listening to

my story. She also shared her experience and opened up about her sadness about the death of her husband.

'I felt guilty that sometimes I forgot about him,' Christine had said.

'We all need to move on,' I said.

Christine looked at me, and slowly she asked, 'Does Ryan know about your past?'

'No.' I took a deep breath. 'And I would be grateful if you could keep it between us.'

Christine raised her eyebrows, looking surprised. 'Why?'

'I don't like to mix my personal and professional life.'

'But Ryan is not like others – you two...' She paused and carefully studied my face. 'You two had the same childhood.'

I lightly shook my head. 'No, we are not the same. He has you—'

Christine interrupted. 'And you will have him. Don't be afraid, Anna, don't push him away. If you get to know him, maybe one day, you can find that peace yourself.'

★ ★ ★ ★

I looked at Ryan through the mirror back and forth, checking all the details on his face to see if it was photo-shoot ready. 'Are you ready?' I said.

'Yep.' He lifted a sunshine smile, one that would kill all his fans.

We went out of the changing room to the studio. The management of an advertising agency and the commercial clients were already there.

'Mr Norton.' Ken from the agency came over and reached for a handshake.

'Call me Ryan.'

'Ryan, let me introduce you to Mark Kay. He is the marketing director of Aqui.'

After the brief introduction, the shooting began.

Each flash had Ryan change his posture slightly. Sometimes his hand, his shoulder or his leg. He looked as if he was a professional model.

Oh yes, he was a model before he joined the company.

The self-introduction we'd had at his aunt's restaurant came back to me. But seeing him modelling in real life was so much better than listening to it.

Each move was smooth and natural, and his gestures and posture were elegant. With that medium-built body, he would be a perfect supermodel.

'The photos are amazing,' Ken said to Ryan when the shoot finished.

The important people gathered around the computer behind the set, checking the eight hundred photos they had taken.

I walked over to Ken and thanked him for the opportunity for Ryan and Magnum.

We left the studio after a quick shake of hands.

'I see why you made it to the magazine,' I said to Ryan when we got into the car.

'What do you mean?'

'Did you learn modelling posture?'

He thought about that and smiled. 'You think I am good?'

'Not bad.' I teased.

He snorted. 'Thanks, that's encouraging. But I didn't go to a school to learn if that's what you are asking.' He took out a bottle of water and sipped.

My eyes widened with disbelief. 'But that was professional modelling in there.'

'Am I that good?' He arched his brow. 'Well, I watched a YouTube of another professional model. I guess I learned from them.' He passed me his bottle of water. 'Water?'

My gaze landed on the bottleneck, which happened to be where his lips had just touched. Overlapping mine on top, wouldn't it become an indirect kiss? An image of us kissing caused my whole body to flush. I shook my head to reject his offer as well as to throw away the forbidden thought.

'You have talent.' I diverted my attention back to his career. 'Why not stay in modelling?'

'More money as a singer.' He laughed.

I rolled my eyes. 'I thought you sang out of passion.'

He burst into laughter. 'Of course I do, you do need to have passion to be a singer, but the money is motivation.'

'Well, I'll see how passionate you are in thirty minutes.'

'We are going to record my new song!' Instantly, his eyes sparkled. The angelic face was lifted in excitement.

I suddenly felt a bit guilty because I hadn't listened to his song yet as promised.

'You will like the new album.' He smiled. 'I think it's better than the previous one.'

I nodded and looked down at my phone.

The silence went on for a minute and then Ryan cried out, 'You still haven't listened to my album!'

I looked up at him and met his disappointed gaze. 'I did,' I lied.

'What's the name of the album?'

'*Gone Again.*' That was all I could remember. I prayed he would not follow up with other questions.

'What's the name of the first song?'

'Come on, I only listen to the music, I don't study the details,' I said.

He squinted. 'The truth will eventually come out.'

'Yeah, and we shall condemn and execute the dishonest ones.'

Ryan thought for a few seconds, looking muddled. '*Macbeth*?' he asked.

'No.' I faintly twitched a smile. 'Anna Bell.'

The straight-faced Ryan ended up guffawing throughout the ride.

When we got to the recording studio, Ryan took charge of guiding me to studio one. He pointed the way to the vending machine and the bathroom.

'You know your way around.' I teased.

He flashed me a smile. The shoot today seemed not to have affected him; his energy was still up to the roof.

We went into a room full of music recording equipment, and a man in his thirties dressed in an oversized white T-shirt and wide trousers came over to greet us. 'Ryan!'

'Josh.' They gave each other a big hug and Ryan introduced me to him.

Our company was very calculating when discussing staff salary and benefits. But they did put lots of their budget and resources into music making. That was why when they hired experienced music producers like Josh they never blinked, even if it was extremely costly.

'Are you ready to make another hit?'

Ryan gave his signature sunshine smile. 'Not unless it's with you.'

Josh rolled his eyes but couldn't hide the big smile on his face. 'You are a sweet talker, aren't you?' Josh looked at me with a serious face. 'Be careful of him.'

I laughed. 'No worries, I am immune to all his words.'

'Hey, you two!' Ryan laughed.

Josh and I teased Ryan a little bit more then we began recording.

Today they were recording the first song of an album that would be released on Spotify and other music platforms.

Ryan walked out of the room and went into the one next door, which was behind a glass wall.

He stood behind a mic and put on big headphones. Josh was testing the mic from our room and he asked Ryan whether he could hear his voice over the mic. Ryan held up a thumb.

When everything was set, Josh did a final check.

During that time, Ryan shot a gaze at me. I held up a thumb and returned a grin. I thought he would smile back, but he didn't. Instead he kept his stare on me until the music started.

My body froze when he sang, and goosebumps rose on my skin.

An unshakable sadness in his voice filled the air. I wasn't an expert in music, yet his soothing voice was deep and comforting. Each word in the song invaded my mind, occupied my brain and unlocked all my gloomy memories from the past.

CHAPTER TEN

> We were so close, like a perfect pair
> But it's all changed, I'm no longer there
> The night lying on the white fur
> We both end up with scars

I listened carefully to every word in the lyrics, and memories of Chris quietly sneaked into my head. Tears floated in my eyes, waiting for a chance to fall down my cheeks. When I couldn't breathe through my nose, a warning alert came into my head. I slowly took out my mobile and tried to take away my focus on his song. Before he finished the last line, I had successfully stopped the falling of tears.

Ryan came out of the recording room and into our room.

'How was it?' he asked.

I looked up after I finished reading an email from my manager.

'Great!' I nodded with a smile. 'Your voice is beautiful,' I said sincerely, but I could not say anymore, otherwise my lacrimal gland would start working again.

Ryan dropped his shoulders when he saw my mobile. 'Really?'

'Of course.' I nodded again.

'It's great,' Josh said. 'Now I'll polish the song a bit and I'll send a copy to your manager, okay?'

When we got out of the studio together, Ryan still looked disappointed.

'Come on, Ryan.' I smiled. 'I did hear you sing.'

'I know, but you weren't really paying attention to the lyrics.' His downturned mouth and monotone voice screamed despondency. I felt overwhelmed by his insistence on me listening to his song.

'I was,' I said truthfully.

'No, you weren't. You were playing with your phone.' He accelerated his walking speed.

I looked at his back and breathed out a sigh.

'We were so close, like a perfect pair. But it's all changed, I'm no longer there…' I tried to sing the lyrics, but my voice wasn't really made for singing; it sounded like a cats' chorus.

Ryan stopped and turned around to me. He widened his eyes and smiled. But quickly he burst into laughter. 'That's how you sing?' He chortled with glee at my voice.

'If I could sing, you would be back to the modelling business,' I retorted.

'Of course I would.' He tried to act serious yet fell back to laughter in less than a second.

'Anyway, it's six o'clock now and I am officially off work.' I walked away and left him where he was.

He ran towards me and walked at the same speed as I did. 'Hey, do you want to hang around together this weekend?'

I glanced at him. 'Depends.'

'Why?'

'I'm fussy about the places I go at the weekend.'

'How about going to the zoo? We can see some cool animals.'

'How cool?' His suggestion was captivating but I had to act cool.

'The king of the jungle isn't cool?'

'You mean the lion?'

He nodded and sang a song from *The Lion King*.

I laughed.

'If that doesn't satisfy you, there are also goats.' He put his finger on his head like a goat horn. 'Or a giraffe – you can feed them to see their long tongue.' He put his hand in front of his lips like a long tongue. 'Or a monkey, you can see them swing around.' He held up his hands and acted like a monkey.

'You know if you were out of work, you could try acting...' An image of Chris rose in my mind, and an alert rang in my ear.

'What did you say?' Ryan was immersed in acting animals and wasn't paying attention to my words.

'Nothing,' I said.

He asked, 'So what do you think?'

'Um...' I muttered. 'Maybe next time.'

He pouted his lips, showing me his disappointment, but I thought it was better to keep a distance.

'Why?' he asked.

'I've got something to do,' I explained. Well, it was just some damn excuse.

He didn't follow up with any questions.

Have you ever had an experience where someone praised a place and made you want to go there? Guess what? It happened to me.

On Saturday, the *Lion King* song was playing in my head for the whole morning, giving me a huge urge to visit the zoo.

But should I invite Ryan?

An image of Chris appeared again.

Maybe not.

I put on a T-shirt and jeans and set off to London Zoo.

The park was filled with parents and kids. I bought an ice cream, leisurely walked around the zoo, and enjoyed the monkeys throwing bananas, two giraffes neck-swinging with their companion, and a bird pooping on a tourist's head.

A tickling feeling had me turn around. A big white dog was licking my leg, and his long fur and big eyes were the same as Snowball's. I gazed up and saw an old couple smiling at me; they must have been the dog's owners. I chatted with them for a while and petted their dog. That gorgeous white fur and cute round eyes reminded me of Snowball's sweetness. A memory that should have been buried slowly emerged.

A roar woke me from my deep thinking; I looked over. A lion was standing on a rock growling. Everyone raised their mobile to capture this fierce cat.

'So, the thing you've got to do is to come here but without me.' A familiar voice rose above my head.

I turned and saw a stranger; he was six feet tall with mid-length messy black hair; he was wearing a hat and sunglasses that covered half his face. I could even see my confusion in a reflection on his glasses.

'It's me.' The man slid down his sunglasses and exposed his blue eyes.

'Ryan?' I whispered.

He nodded.

'What is it with your hair?'

'It's my disguise.'

The dull black, synthetic fibre that sat on his head was tangled and tousled like he had just got out of bed. This hilarious prop made me laugh like a drain.

When I finally calmed down, I asked, 'How come you're here?'

'I was going to ask you the same question. I told you I wanted to go to the zoo. What's your excuse?'

Time to come clean.

'Well, you're a great PR for the zoo. I was moved by the *Lion King* song you sang. So I came to check out the majestic...'

He chuckled.

After that, we walked around the zoo together. Ryan knew his way around; he was probably some sort of loyal visitor. He knew where each type of animal was kept; he even knew the location of the toilets and food trucks.

'Do you have an annual pass?' I asked.

Ryan laughed. 'Yeah, yeah, I like the zoo so I come here once a month.'

'Why be a singer when you can be a zoo keeper.' I laughed and dropped myself on a grass field in the park.

Ryan sat next to me and sent me a sheepish smile. 'No,

it's just that this was the last place I came to with my parents before they died.'

Like a virus, the word froze my brain, stopping it from forming any words. I should have come up with some comforting phrases or compassionate words, but my poor communication skills diverted me in other directions.

'Oh...' I said, or some such sound. It was meaningless but possibly the sole response I could give. Seconds went by, and my introvert instinct sent me a dead-air alert. I panicked.

Ryan studied me and eventually burst into laughter. I secretly let a breath out because the awkward moment didn't come as expected.

'Sorry, I've brought up my sad story again.' He giggled. 'My bad.'

'It's fine,' I said. 'Let it out if you want ... I'm here to listen.' I knew I should have been keeping my distance but I was doing the opposite.

Ryan looked me in the eyes for a second and then broke eye contact.

'My mum and dad were both university professors. I still remember they kept reminding me to study hard to get a good job. So I always wonder what would they think of me now being a singer.'

He hunched forward as if he had shut himself off from everyone. The overwhelming sorrow blurred my vision; I took a deep breath and carefully exhaled my sadness.

Speaking was useless, and a hug wouldn't help. Doing nothing was doing the right thing. That was what I felt, what I'd learned.

Silence was my best friend, but I didn't want it to last forever.

After a lot of thinking, I said something ridiculous. 'I think they would wonder why your hair is such a disaster.'

What's wrong with me?

My lousy joke led to more silence. While I was biting my brain for making a fool of myself, Ryan burst into laughter.

'It's the only wig I have.' He giggled.

'Well, you could at least find a normal one.'

'I was hoping you could help me with it.'

'What? So the reason you invited me was to straighten your hair?' I pretended to be angry.

'Yes, and then I can buy you ice cream as a tip.'

'Thank you, how thoughtful.'

We both laughed until we were in tears.

'How about next weekend, do you want to go out with me?' Ryan asked.

'A "date" kind of go out?' I asked.

Ryan's eyes and thoughts were shielded behind his sunglasses, and all I could see was my reflection. Slowly, a corner of his lips lifted and twisted into a bad-boy grin. 'Would you go out on a date with me, Anna?'

If I needed to describe Ryan, I would have said he's a sunny boy, bright and warm, and I could never imagine him with a seductive smile, so evil and irresistible.

But I needed to keep my distance; distance was good.

'Nope, we are co-workers, we can't date each other.'

The evil grin quickly dropped to a disappointed pout. 'Fine, not a date. Just hang around like colleagues.'

I looked at that baby-face and burst into laughter.

'Well...' I hesitated.

'I can treat you to free food.' He added an incentive to the deal.

The words 'free food' did sound attractive...

Don't push him away.

One day you may find that peace of yours.

Christine's words flashed in my head.

Maybe I should take some advice for once.

'Okay,' I said, 'but if there is no free food I will abandon ship.'

Ryan sighed with relief and shook his head. 'What a rip-off.'

'Hey, you're the one who offered.'

'I know, I know...' He pretended to sniff as he pulled out his wallet and looked at the one ten-pound note.

'I hope you have more than that by next week.' I laughed.

Watching his angel face, I had a strange feeling that I might be walking the wrong path, which might lead to a disaster just like the one before.

★ ★ ★ ★

I liked working with Ryan, not because of his work attitude but because of his personality. He loved to talk, although his non-stop chat made it difficult for people around him to work efficiently. But most of us liked it and didn't complain. Working with him was like having a break from all the busy and tiring jobs.

'If he wants to see his friends, he can.' The hair stylist was talking to Ryan about his boyfriend while doing his hair. 'But whenever I want to go to a friend's house – ha, I'm not allowed.'

Ryan said, 'He cares about you.'

The hairstylist rolled his eyes. 'Hey, no, definitely not. He just doesn't want me to have fun.'

'Maybe he doesn't know your friends, that's all.'

The stylist stared blankly as if his brain had just been rebooted. 'Well...'

'Ah!' Ryan laughed. 'You never introduced him to your friends.'

'Fine, you win.' The stylist sent a sheepish smile. 'I will see how it goes.'

'Keep me in the loop.' Ryan gave him a wink.

After he left, Ryan looked at me, biting his lips.

'Either you have dry lips, or you're seducing me,' I said. 'I can only offer you lip balm at this moment.'

He snorted. 'Neither.'

'What do you want to say then?' I let out a breath, knowing he'd just come up with some weird ideas.

He leaned closer to me. 'You know, I've never met any of your friends.'

'I don't have friends.'

'Everyone has friends.'

I shrugged. 'I am not everyone.'

'Fine.' He smiled. 'But one day I will meet your friends and uncover all your secrets.'

'I don't have any secrets.'

'Balls, everyone has secrets.'

Sometimes I would be amazed by this young boy's maturity; I'd forget he was younger than me.

Talent was not enough in this industry; his communication skills were one of the other reasons that made him a hot number in the music business.

I always teased him for being able to talk his way through his career – he could have a talk show. In his defence he said he enjoyed working with people; that was why he liked talking to them. For an outsider, he was a friendly guy, but I knew underneath that this lonely boy just wanted to grab the love from anyone to fill the gaps in his life. I understood because I was also an orphan, but in contrast I did the opposite. I was afraid to let anyone in because the idea of losing anyone again scared me. What happened between Chris and me justified this.

That was why I needed to remind myself constantly that after one date with Ryan, I had to stop. I could not fall for anyone again – well, at least not in this industry.

On Friday, Jess called for a ladies' night. I was glad she still kept in touch with me since I was just a small potato.

After I finished my work with Ryan, I glammed up slightly and prepared to take off.

'I'll pick you up at eight o'clock tomorrow morning,' Ryan said.

'No need, I can take an Uber.'

'Just give me your address.'

'Fine.' I WhatsApped my address to his phone.

While I was typing, I could feel his gaze on me.

'You look nice, where are you going?' Ryan asked sceptically.

'To see a friend.'

'What friend?'

'A friend I used to work with before.'

Ryan stared at me but said nothing further.

'See you tomorrow!' I said.

At that moment, Ryan seemed a bit strange, but my

hungry tummy quickly dragged me away, giving me no time to be concerned about him.

* * * *

When I got out of Magnum, I went straight to the restaurant to meet Jess. She was already in a private booth, and she greeted me with a warm hug.

It had been a while since I had seen her, not that we didn't chat on WhatsApp, but physically seeing her gave me a thrill. I wanted to tell her everything, but then I realised not everything could be shared.

'So how is Ryan Norton?' Jess asked after ordering her food. A hint of jealousy vibrated in her voice, but it was probably my imagination. I didn't give it any thought because an image of Ryan's evil smile was flipping in my memory book. Thinking of it sped up my heart rate. I took a sip of my drink to flush down any dirty thoughts going on in my head.

'He's all right,' I said in a flat tone, so flat that I would give myself an Oscar.

'Oh, come on, he's hot.' Jess grinned and crossed her arms, not buying what I had said.

'But you're more fun to work with.' The satisfied smile from Jess proved that I had given the right response. 'So how are you?' I asked, trying to shift the focus back to her instead of me. 'How's your new assistant?'

'Well, she's all right,' Jess said with a yawn. 'Doesn't speak much, very focused.'

'That's good, you can do all the talking.' I laughed.

'Thanks, but I prefer watching stand-up comedy than performing it,' she teased.

'And you think you're funny?' I acted confused. 'Really?'

She pinched my arm and made me scream.

'I am bored, Anna,' she said.

'Go find a man.'

She glanced at me with a heavy sigh.

'Oh, come on, it was just one man – it shouldn't ruin your whole life,' I said.

'But I'm scared now.' She looked down to her lap. All of a sudden the mood dropped.

'Well, you have me now,' I said.

'And you can do what?'

'Well, I could investigate whoever you're dating to check whether they're married or have killed someone.' A smile slowly rose from her face, and I added, 'But you have to pay me of course.'

Jess laughed. 'I don't have the money.'

'Yeah, right.' I took out my mobile and showed her the statistics. 'Your album just hit number one on Spotify. Where did all that cash go, Jess? Switzerland?'

She laughed even harder. 'Karen took all of it.'

'Poor you, so how did you afford that new Porsche outside?'

Jess looked out of the window and her gaze landed on a red convertible Porsche – *her* convertible Porsche.

'How did you know?' She widened her eyes.

'Didn't you know I subscribe to gossip magazines?'

'I thought you didn't read gossip?'

'Only after...' My mind froze like a computer, and I quickly dragged my memory of Chris into the recycle bin. 'After I met you,' I said.

Jess burst into laughter.

'So when did you buy that car?' I asked.

'It was a gift.'

'Oh, our Jess found a sugar daddy.' I clapped. 'Good job.'

She burst into laughter again.

Even though our chats were silly and full of nonsense, I loved having this together time with Jess. As time went by, I felt that our friendship was even stronger. I had never been close to anyone, especially in this industry. I lived in a different world to these people, but not Jess.

She was a superstar, yet underneath it, she was just like me, lonely and wanting to find a person who cared about her. Another thing I loved about her was she always kept the conversation easy, never pushed you to the edge or made you uncomfortable, nor would she probe about your private life, which I respected. She liked to be close but kept a reasonable distance.

'So, it's my birthday in three weeks,' she said in a sneaky tone. I felt like something fishy was going on. 'I'm having a party, please come. It's at the Dragon Club, lots of hot guys will be there.'

I rolled my eyes.

'Oh, come on, you have to come,' Jess said.

'Fine, send me the time and address.'

'Yeah!' Jess cheered. 'It will be fun.' She gave me a goofy smile.

Something was odd about this, but our food had arrived, so I threw my concerns away. I needed to concentrate on food right now.

The evening was terrific; we had a great dinner, and a great catch-up on recent events – well, except for the part at the zoo and the 'hang-around' activity with Ryan – everything was perfect.

CHAPTER ELEVEN

The next day I woke up bright and shiny. Fortunately, I didn't drink too much with Jess the night before, so I didn't need to deal with a hangover the next morning, especially when Ryan arrived at exactly 8 a.m.

I rushed out with light make-up. I didn't want to overdress, so I wore a loose-fit white T-shirt and denim shorts.

'You're on time,' I said.

'Of course, it's our first *hang-around* activity.' Ryan on the other hand, was wearing a black shirt with rolled-up sleeves and blue jeans. His big sunglasses covered half his face, but I was disappointed not to see him in his wig.

'No wig today?'

'We won't be seeing a lot of people.' He smiled. 'Breakfast?'

'Free?'

Ryan rolled his eyes and nodded. 'Yeah, yeah, yeah, all on me today.'

He drove us to his aunt's restaurant and we were escorted to our usual seat.

Christine came over to take our order. 'Good morning, everyone.' This was the first time I realised she and Ryan had the same soft blue eyes, and even the angelic smile was very similar.

'Good morning, Christine,' I said.

'We need to be fed,' Ryan said.

'No problem. You can order whatever you want, but...' Christine smiled at him. 'You better pay for whatever you have.'

Ryan laughed. 'Is it not free? You own this place.'

'Well, perhaps. But aren't you guys on a date? You should pay for Anna and yourself.' She winked at me. 'It is a gentlemanly gesture.'

Her words made me worried. 'Oh, no, we're—'

'We are not on a date, we're just *hanging around* like colleagues,' Ryan said.

'Oh.' Christine looked at us back and forth. 'As indeed you are.' She snickered.

The misunderstanding made me speechless, and I closed my eyes hoping this would go away soon.

After we ordered our breakfast, I said, 'Now your aunt thinks we're on a date.'

Ryan laughed. 'So?'

'We're not on a date.'

'Well, you're not on a date, but I am.' He laughed. 'You can think what you want, but I can do the same.'

I smile resignedly, feeling defeated.

'Never mind,' I said, thinking this would be the last time I *hung around* with him.

Our amazing breakfast arrived. Ryan had ordered an

Italian baked egg and sausage, whereas I ordered an amazing-looking frittata; the combination of melted cheese, eggs and bacon was just the best thing to start the day.

※ ※ ※ ※

'Where are we going exactly?' I asked after we returned to his car.

'You will know soon.'

An hour later, he stopped in front of a house and I could see an animal farm behind it. A man in his fifties came out from the house and welcomed us.

'Ryan!' They hugged each other. 'This must be Miss Bell.' He turned to me and hugged me too. 'I'm Steve. Nice to meet you.'

I smiled in confusion. 'Nice to meet you too.'

'Come on in,' Steve said.

'How come he knows my name? Who is he?' I whispered to Ryan. He didn't reply but instead threw me a smile.

We followed Steve to his living room, and he disappeared somewhere.

Ryan suggested I sit on an armchair.

'Why?' I questioned. 'What are you going to do?'

He took off his sunglasses and gave me a warm smile. 'Trust me.' He took out a handkerchief from his pocket. 'I need to cover your eyes first.'

'Why?' Covering my eyes worried me.

'Do you trust me?'

My silence gave him the green light to blindfold me. With my vision gone, an isolated feeling grew inside me. Not that I was scared of this feeling, but it was more like I'd got used to it. I'd been alone all my life, and even when I was with Chris, I often felt isolated.

Suddenly, a soft and warm object landed on my lap. I grabbed hold of it without thinking. A small and furry object brushed my palm, its tail wagging like a helicopter.

Then, another soft object landed on my lap and this one licked my hand. I knew what they were.

'Oh!' I screamed when more and more of them landed on my lap. 'I need to see them, Ryan!'

Ryan took away the handkerchief and the sudden light blurred my vision. After my eyes adjusted, I saw eight puppies sitting on my lap. They were Labradors.

I screamed out my joy and made an effort to pet each of them. Some of them gave me a tiny weeping noise, while some tried to climb on me.

'Am I in heaven?' I cried.

Ryan laughed and took a picture of me.

Then I realised Steve was standing next to him.

'I'm so sorry.' I felt embarrassed but I had no intention of letting any of the puppies go. 'They are adorable!' I cupped one puppy in my hand and cuddled it.

'No worries. You have fun there. I'll get you some drinks.' The man chuckled. 'Lemonade or wine?'

'Wine, yes please!' I said with excitement.

I felt a long stare from Ryan, but I didn't care. The puppies were like a stimulant, keeping my energy high. I wasn't interested in anything else.

'Lemonade for me, thanks.' Ryan chuckled.

Steve disappeared to the kitchen.

I held up another puppy and kissed him. The puppy replied with a cute high-pitched whine.

'You like my kisses?' I said in a child's voice and gave him another kiss.

Ryan kneeled next to me and petted the puppy I'd just kissed. 'Cute.'

'Yes, they are...' I turned my head and realised he'd been looking at me all this time. His stare heated my body like a fire and stimulated my blood to travel to my head at lightning speed. I felt my cheeks burning and a long-gone feeling had returned. I broke the eye contact to pull the plug, wanting to turn all my feelings for him off like a switch.

I glued my eyes on the puppies and petted them gently. Ryan leaned closer, and his mild cologne took over my mind. He moved his hand over to the puppy that I was petting, and when our fingers touched, he gently locked my fingers with his.

His soft touch blanked out my mind. I thought he was playing some trick, but when I saw the tenderness in his gaze, I knew he was not messing with me. A smile gradually lifted on his face. I wanted to look away, but his smile locked my soul to him. It felt like we had entered another space, a space with only the two of us.

The sound of footsteps brought us back to real life. Steve was standing in front of us with our drinks. Our hands broke apart.

'Sorry, did I interrupt anything?' he said with a sneaky smile.

I took the time to cool down the heat in my face.

'Only a sleeping puppy.' Ryan pointed to one that was waking and yawning.

Steve laughed. 'They will all be awake in a minute anyway. It's lunchtime for them.'

He handed us the drinks and then started waving a bag.

The sound of plastic woke all eight puppies, and they all looked alertly in the same direction. Three seconds later they jumped off my lap and followed Steve to the kitchen.

Ryan and I joined Steve to enjoy the scene of eight puppies eating.

After we left Steve's house, we set off to our third destination.

'How did you know I like dogs?' I asked.

'You have one on your screensaver.' Ryan pointed to my phone.

A big white dog was boldly displayed on my screen. Snowball's image was still stored on my phone, the only link to Chris I hadn't removed.

'Is that your dog?' Ryan asked.

My guilty conscience silenced me. An urge to tell him the truth came into my mind, but the words clogged in my throat.

'Nope, just a random dog,' I said after a weird long pause that I prayed Ryan didn't notice.

He returned a smile without asking any further.

After a long drive, the car stopped in front of a cottage. Ryan got out of the car and walked toward the house.

'Where are we?' I followed him imagining there would be another dog or cat jumping out. I secretly hoped for a cat because I hadn't petted a cat for a long time.

Ryan stopped by the door and waited for me to catch up.

'Welcome to my home.' He opened the door as he spoke.

I popped my head inside the house and expected to see a

warm and beautiful home, but instead, the house was empty, cold and filled with dust.

'There's nothing here.' I grumbled like a teenager.

'It was my home before my parents passed away,' he said.

My jaw dropped; the sudden change of vibe left me speechless. But before my mind ran for the panic button, Ryan quickly added, 'Sorry, I'm talking about my dead parents again. But...' His glance lingered on my face as he shortened his distance from me. 'I want you to know everything about me.' His sincere expression made my body feel hot, and my knees turn weak. I pretended to stroll around the house, avoiding eye contact, hoping this would calm me. But he kept following me. Eventually, I gave up on the home viewing and returned to the front door.

'So, do you always bring girls here?' I grinned.

'Yes,' he answered firmly.

My plan was to tease him, but the sincerity in his eyes made my guilt take off like a rocket. The genuine smile on his face was like proof of my hidden secret, a repressing self-defence that I used to hide my vulnerable self. His attitude and words had dismantled my safety wall piece by piece. I wanted to run away from him.

'How many have there been then?' I tried to hide my anxiety under a fake laugh.

'Three girlfriends,' he said clearly with no hesitation. 'How about you?'

'Just three? Really?' I made an effort to spin the topic back to him.

He paused, and a few seconds later, that evil smile returned.

'Yes, three.' He slowly moved closer to me.

He cupped my cheek with one hand. 'What are you hiding? Why won't you let me in?' He was so close to me that I could feel his every breath, and the gentleness of his voice softly calmed my nerves. I gazed up, and time just froze when our eyes locked.

Ryan slowly lowered his head and landed his lips on mine. The warmth of his flesh spread through my veins, and the taste of caring and trust wiped out my mind. I begged myself to push him away, but my arms ignored my warning and hugged him tighter. I returned his kiss, let his tongue explore my inner self and suck away my defensive bars one by one. We were like fire; if he hadn't stopped, we would have probably done it right there.

The room was quiet; the only noise was the sound of our breath.

I buried my head in his chest, not willing to disclose the desire in my eyes. We hugged each other tight.

'Anna.' Ryan broke the silence; his soft tone gently reached my ears. 'Will you be my girlfriend?'

CHAPTER TWELVE

'What?' Ryan widened his eyes as he shrieked. 'Rules?'

'Yes.' I flashed him a smile. 'We need to set some rules if we are going to be a couple.'

It was overwhelming when Ryan asked me to be his girlfriend; it blanked my mind, but then I said yes with the heat still pumping through my body. When I cooled down, unexpectedly I had no regrets about my decision. But I did have some concerns about dating a celebrity, *again*. I had too many bad memories. So, after Ryan had driven me home that evening, I had lain on my bed and begun to imagine all the possible bad outcomes. My agitated nerves had warned me not to follow in the footsteps of my previous relationship. Something had to be different. After a night of serious consideration, I had devised a genius idea, which Ryan hated.

'Rule number one, we can't tell anyone.'

'Like the fight club?' He chuckled.

'Don't joke about our rules.' I frowned at him. 'Rule number two, no kissing or hugging in public.'

Ryan nodded.

'Rule number three, no sleepovers at each other's house.'

Ryan squinted.

'Just to be cautious,' I added before he could question further. He digested my words and nodded unwillingly.

'Last rule.'

'Thank God.' Ryan lifted his head and raised his hand in the air.

'No sex.'

'What?' He groaned with his blue eyes wide. 'Forever?'

'Of course not, just when we're ready.'

'Well, I am ready.' He grabbed my waist and pulled me towards him. When our eyes met, he lowered his head and shot me hundreds of kisses on my face and lips.

'Breaking rule number two.' I giggled out his 'crime' while my hand faked pushing him away.

Although he didn't think the rules were necessary, in the end, he still agreed to comply with them.

Everyone knew dating a co-worker could be troublesome, but on the bright side it could be heavenly bliss.

'Anna, here are the clothes for Ryan. Let us know when he's ready.' A handsome young PA passed me a pile of designer clothes. 'See you later.'

I closed the door behind me and put the clothes on the table in the changing room. A pair of arms wrapped around my waist from behind. I turned my head to the owner of those arms, and before I could say anything, a kiss fell on my cheek.

'Hey,' I shouted.

'Not breaking rule number two.' He pointed to the empty room. 'No one is here.'

'But people might walk in on us.'

'Relax...'

I sighed, knowing that I might have been slightly over-agitated.

It was sweet whenever Ryan gave me a sudden kiss in public, but it was also nerve-racking.

'So what are we doing tonight?' Ryan picked up a shirt and a pair of jeans from the pile of clothes; he quickly examined them and smiled at the ones he'd picked. He walked in front of the mirror and took off his T-shirt. The lightbulbs on the side of the mirror were so bright that I didn't have clear sight of his face, but only a silhouette of his body. Every tress of his hair was like gold thread; he shone like an angel and that God-made muscular figure was fully captured in my eyes.

My lips widened slightly, and the taste of his torso in my imagination was so good that the tip of my tongue needed to pop out and confirm. I could feel the blood in my veins pumping a disco beat.

I guessed my silence caught Ryan's attention. But the bright light made it difficult for me to see his face. From his movement, I guessed he had turned around. He slowly walked towards me. When he stood just one foot away from me, I could faintly see that evil grin on his face.

He cupped my face in his palm, rubbing my cheeks gently. 'Do you always look at guys like this?'

'What?'

He looked into my eyes, my soul. 'Don't,' he whispered as he lowered his head and kissed me. I felt the heat from my stomach rising again; my limbs turned weak. 'Don't you dare to look at other guys like that, okay?' he said in a warning tone. I didn't know what he was talking about, but I nodded so that we could continue our kiss.

★ ★ ★

'Are you free tonight?' Ryan asked after the interview.

I was packing my work case and preparing to leave. 'Not tonight, why?'

'Where are you going?' Ryan looked sceptical.

'Just meeting a friend.' I snorted.

'What kind of friend?' he asked with a straight face like a police officer as if I was planning something evil.

'A female friend I used to work with.' I held my palm up. 'What is this? An interrogation?' I huffed.

He squinted his eyes and released a laugh when he couldn't hold the expression anymore.

'You are the worst interrogator.' I laughed.

'If I put on a real mask, you would be petrified.' He grabbed me around the waist and landed lots of kisses on my cheeks. 'I'll see you tomorrow,' he said as he walked out of the changing room.

★ ★ ★

I went home to take a quick shower and dress for the party. Then I saw the WhatsApp reminder from Jess. I smiled and left the house.

The party was at a club in town; celebrities and

executives from our company approached the club from across the road. Cameras were flashing like lightning at the entrance, and I walked quickly to avoid being snapped.

The club was massive with a huge round dance floor in the centre and a circular bar.

It was almost eleven o'clock when I arrived, and people were dancing and drinking. I searched for Jess in the sea of guests, and finally I spotted her on the dance floor with a guy. I walked towards her, and she was so happy to see me, she greeted me with a big hug and pulled me to the bar. The bartender handed me a tequila shot, and then we drank it like water.

A minute later, I was given another shot, Jess shouted 'bottoms up', and I finished my second round.

'No more.' I stopped her before she handed me a third.

'Don't be a pussy!' Jess teased. 'You won't be wasted just with two...' Jess paused and focused on a person behind me.

I turned around and saw a cute-looking guy. He was in his early thirties, medium built and tanned. His blond hair looked newly cut and was neatly slicked back. Jess walked over and hugged him. Soon after, she brought him over to me.

'Anna, meet Duke!' She gave me a goofy smile. 'Duke, meet Anna. You are both into styling, discuss!'

Before I could react, she ran off giggling like a teenager.

Duke saw the confusion on my face and laughed. 'She's trying to set us up.'

'What?' I shouted and scanned the dance floor to find Jess. Then I thought of Ryan, and his baby face came into my mind.

'So, you're a make-up artist?' Duke asked.

I pulled myself back into the bar. 'Yes, and you? Jess just mentioned you're into styling too?'

'Yes, I am a hairdresser. I'm currently under contract with F/A.'

'Oh, woah, is that where you met Jess?'

'Yeah, I met her last month,' Duke said. 'So does she like to act as cupid and go around setting people up?'

'Um, I am not sure.' I chuckled. 'But if that offended you, I apologise for her.'

'No, I am glad she did,' Duke answered with a smile in his eyes.

A strange feeling rose in my guts. Was he hitting on me?

'So, when will you be free?' he asked.

Asking me out so fast?

'Um...' I mumbled, trying to think of an excuse that wouldn't hurt him.

'Relax, I just want to do your hair.' He chuckled.

I didn't know whether that was an excuse, but I sure would have loved to have my hair done by a star hairdresser.

'Will it break the bank?' I smirked.

'It will be affordable.' He smiled. 'Give me your number.'

He pulled out his phone and we exchanged numbers.

We chatted for a while, mostly about work. I felt that we liked similar styles and clothing – minimal, earthy tones. It was interesting that he also liked pop art; the use of bold colours especially fascinated him. He felt like an old friend with lots to catch up on.

'You know, Anna ... I would love to chat more with you but I have an early shoot tomorrow,' Duke said.

'No worries, go home. I understand the pain of early rising.' I smiled.

Duke looked at me.

'What's wrong?' I tilted my head to the side, wondering.

'I hope I can see you again.' The sincerity in his eyes made me nervous. I was out of words so I nodded my head, hoping he didn't notice my sudden change of attitude.

After Duke left, I went to the bathroom for a little freshen-up. When I came out, a strong hand grabbed me and led me to a quiet corner of the bar.

The suddenness sped up my heartbeat and scared the hell out of me; I tried to get rid of the hand on my arm. And while I was trying to break away from the intruder's hand, I saw the deep blue eyes.

'Ryan?' I shouted. 'How come—'

'What were you doing?' Ryan sounded enraged.

'I told you I was meeting friends. It's Jess's birthday today.' I softened my voice, trying to calm his anger.

But it didn't seem to be working. Ryan was still angry.

'Really? Funny that – I don't see Jess around but only you flirting with that creep.'

'What creep?' I tried to rewind time. The only person his sentence could refer to was Duke. 'You mean Duke?' I chuckled. 'I wasn't flirting with him.'

'Yeah? Well, the way he looked at you is flirting with you.' Ryan pouted like a furious baby.

'Well...' I slowly raised my hand and gently slid my fingertips across his chest. 'I can tell you that's not how I flirt.' I grinned and flashed him a seductive glance.

I guess my flirting worked. A smile faintly rose on his face.

Knowing Ryan had cooled down a bit, I took the opportunity to explain. 'It's just Jess's joke.' I smiled. 'She was trying to match us up.' Before Ryan could be angry, I added, 'But I'll tell her I am seeing someone.'

'Someone?' Ryan repeated my word in an incensed tone.

'Come on, Ryan. Rule number one,' I pleaded in a sweet soft voice.

Finally, he agreed, but I had to tell Jess tonight.

The dance floor was packed with people, and dozens of couples were dancing face to face, chest on chest. It wasn't easy to get past them while searching for Jess. In the end, I found her at the back of the dance floor. I pulled her to one side and tried to explain my situation.

'Oh my God, who's the lucky guy?' she squealed with surprise. Her eyes sparkled and shone after I told her I was seeing someone.

'Just some guy,' I replied. 'Please tell Duke I am sorry. It's my fault, I should have told him just now.'

'Forget about Duke, just tell me who your boyfriend is.' Jess was totally thrilled; she grabbed my shoulder, trying to shake out my answer.

'I can't tell you.'

'Is he a spy?'

'What? No!'

'Is he a billionaire?'

'No.'

'Someone's husband?'

'*No*!'

'Oh come on, you can't leave me hanging like this. Give me something.' Jess pulled a puppy face and was so beautiful and cute.

'It doesn't—'

'Oh my God, it's Ryan!' Jess screamed before I could finish my sentence. She pointed to the other side of the dance floor. I followed her gaze and saw Ryan frowning at us, irritated.

'He really can't pull a poker face.' Jess laughed. 'I'll talk to him, you stay here.'

She left before I could stop her. She passed through the crowd like a snake and spoke to Ryan.

A few minutes later, Ryan shot me a smile and left.

Jess returned to my side and passed me a drink.

'Now, you will have fun with me tonight,' Jess said.

'What did you tell him?' I was sceptical.

Jess took a sip of her wine and flashed me a goofy smile. 'Secret.'

For the next twenty-four hours, no matter how much I begged, the conversation between her and Ryan remained a secret.

CHAPTER THIRTEEN

'Breaking rule number one!' I said.

'It's not my fault, and I didn't say a word.' Ryan shrugged and gave me a sheepish smile. It was true that he hadn't disclosed anything to Jess, but the way he looked at me at the party gave it away.

After Jess had discovered our relationship, she was happy and agreed to keep the secret. I wasn't worried she would spread the news behind our backs because she was a good friend, but I reckoned people would notice if Ryan kept staring at me with all that softness in his eyes, and next time it might be seen by our manager.

'What do you want me to do? It was impossible to turn my head when I saw you flirting with that creep.' Ryan frowned. I was angry but then couldn't resist his jealous cute face. I knew he cared, and it was something that I'd lost with Chris.

'I did not flirt with him. I was just casually talking with a guy who I just met.' I gave him a warm hug. 'I won't talk to him anymore, okay?'

Ryan nodded.

He lowered his head and dropped his lips on mine.

Working as Ryan's assistant was probably the best cover; we could hang out without people questioning it. Sometimes Jess would invite us to her house and let us have some private time.

One day, we were in a changing room in a studio, and Ryan once again went to hug and kiss me.

'We're in our room, why can't I kiss you? There is no one here.' Ryan pulled a long face after I backed away from his kiss.

'This is still a public changing room, other people might walk in,' I argued.

'They'll knock on the door.'

'What if they don't?'

'What if—'

Before Ryan could finish his sentence, someone knocked on the door while opening it at the same time.

'Sorry to interrupt, but here are the shirts for later.' The event assistant passed us the clothing in a hurry and left.

'Don't give me that "I told you" look,' Ryan said, rolling his eyes.

I burst into laughter.

Time was flying in those happy days. But I became sloppy and then our secret romance was no longer a secret.

A couple of months after Jess's party, I bumped into Duke at a studio.

'Anna!'

I turned around and was met with a familiar face.

'Dan...' I tried hard to remember the guy's name. 'Duke!' I wanted to applaud myself for getting the name right.

'How are you?' he said with slight disappointment.

'Great! You?'

'Yeah...' He trailed off. 'I didn't call you—'

'I am sorry, Duke.' I knew where this was going, so I thought it best to come clean before he asked any further. 'I should have told you earlier that I have a boyfriend,' I explained. 'I just started seeing him and it's nothing too stable, so...'

'It's fine. Jess already told me.' Duke smiled and patted my shoulder, reassuring me he was not angry. 'We can still be friends, right?'

'Only if you can give me a discount for a hairdo.' I laughed.

He nodded. 'Just text me before you visit my store, and I will get you sorted.' He smiled. 'Anyway, I've got to run.' He waved me goodbye as he left.

Then I remembered I was also in a hurry, so I ran to Ryan's changing room.

'Sorry I'm late.' I rushed into the room and saw Ryan on the phone.

'Sure, I'll let her know...' He pointed at the corner.

Five different shirts were hanging on the rack. They were the same colour but in different patterns. I held them up one by one to pick the best one for the shoot today.

'Yes, okay...' Ryan continued talking on his phone and came up behind me. I held up one of the shirts to indicate my choice. He gave it a nod, grabbed the shirt and tossed it on the sofa.

The next second, he grabbed my waist and pulled me to him, hugging me tight.

'Okay, Karen, yeah...' After Ryan hung up, he put his head on my shoulder and let out a long sigh.

'What does she want?' I raked one hand into his hair and let my fingers feel the silky soft texture.

'She asked you to stop by tomorrow.'

'Okay, by the way, the shirt for later—'

His lips landed on mine, interrupting my words.

'Ryan!' I pulled away quickly but Ryan refused to let go of my waist.

'Come on, no one's here,' he said and planted another kiss on me. His angelic smile had softened my guard. I let him kiss me again and again until I heard someone gasp.

Ryan and I both looked to the side and saw a guy standing next to the door. Duke widened his eyes as if he'd seen a ghost; he had his mouth open but no words came out. The scene had probably drained the blood out from his body – he turned pale.

'Duke!' I groaned in panic, knowing he might expose our secret. I quickly ran through a list of excuses in my head, trying to make up a story for this incident. But nothing could ever cover this up.

The three of us just quietly stood there, no doubt all thinking about how to get out of this awkward moment.

Ryan broke the silence. 'Please don't tell anyone.'

Duke looked at us back and forth, opened his mouth to say something but just sighed.

'The photo shoot will start in fifteen minutes. I think you guys better get ready,' he said.

I looked at Ryan and pointed at the shirt. 'Okay, you get changed now. I'll wait for you outside.'

Duke and I walked out of the changing room. I grabbed his arm after the door was shut. 'Duke.'

He looked at me quietly and thoughtfully.

'Please keep the secret for me,' I begged.

'You are not serious about him, right?'

I was quite offended by the tone of his voice. But the last thing I wanted was to irritate him and give him an excuse to spread my secret to the world.

'Yes, I am,' I said.

He laughed contemptuously. 'Come on, Anna.' He leaned closer and grabbed my shoulder. 'He is not serious and you know that! Those people like to mess with us, they'll dump us faster than their new song release.'

I stared at him, not taking in any of his words.

My absence of response must have signalled my anger. He looked away and gave out a long sigh.

'Sorry, Anna, I know it's not my place to say anything. But listen to me.' He thought for a second, and a glimpse of sadness sparked through his eyes. His palm was on my shoulder, like a friend. 'You will regret it. So don't fall for him. I don't want you to get hurt.'

His sorrowful expression made me realise the reason for this extreme reaction was probably due to his past. But his experience was not mine; it was not fair for him to judge Ryan the same way as the person who had hurt him.

'I understand and am very grateful for your care.' I patted him on his shoulder. 'But Ryan will not hurt me. I believe in him.' Never in my life had I been so sure and trusting of someone.

Duke paused and finally released a smile. 'Okay, in that case, I hope you'll be happy.'

We hugged and he left for his next job.

I looked at my watch and panicked because Ryan should be in the studio now. I knocked on the door to check if he was ready.

When he opened the door, he fell on me, hugging me tight.

'I love you, Anna,' he whispered in my ear.

CHAPTER FOURTEEN

As an orphan, I always hid my thoughts and feelings. Some psychologists said this was a sort of self-defence. Shield yourself, put up a guard, show no weakness, make yourself an unbreakable warrior, and in this way, no one would be able to hurt you. I had been doing this throughout my life and I was proud to say it had led me to a promising career. With this track record, I believed it was the only way to success, that once I showed my vulnerable side, every bit of my hard work would be crushed into dust, and never again would I see the sun in this industry.

Since my secret was exposed, I felt like someone was hiding in an alley with a knife, planning to stab me. My insecurity made me paranoid. I browsed the news every morning, checking all news related to Ryan just to be sure our secret remained so. My life now depended on Duke; if he wanted me to disappear, he could just spread the news and I wouldn't be seen again.

But it never happened.

I guessed I owed that guy a lot.

'It's fine,' Jess said. 'Duke has been in this place long enough, he knows the rules. He won't tell anyone, don't worry.' She popped a grape in her mouth.

I looked at her and Ryan back and forth, wondering whether I had overthought it.

'Don't worry, we'll be fine.' Ryan also ate a grape, but judging by his lemon face, I decided not to touch any.

'Just forget about it and get on with your life,' Jess said. 'You can't spend all day long thinking about something that hasn't happened.'

'Agreed.' Ryan laughed. 'You haven't seen her in the past week – she's been like some detective searching every website for hints of our news.'

Just for a second, my mind froze.

A long-forgotten memory that was buried underground was knocking on my door.

It had been a while since I was called 'detective', and an image of myself laughing with Chris re-emerged in my mind.

'How's Detective Anna today?' The olive eyes smile with his voice.

I thought I had forgotten about him and our past, but I underestimated my brain. Just one word, his voice and smile could magically reappear in my head.

'Anna!' Ryan looked concerned. 'Are you okay?'

My mind had wandered away for a while. I nodded and flashed him a smile to reassure him.

'Hey, do you guys want to watch a movie?' Jess asked.

'Sure, we can check out Netflix,' I said, searching for the remote.

'No! I mean at the cinema.'

'Cinema?' I said. 'Come on, you know we are trying to keep our secret.'

'It's fine, we can go in after the lights go down. No one will notice. Besides, we are all going together, not just you two.' She grabbed my hand and swung it like a child begging for a present.

'No.'

'Why...?' Jess pulled a sour face; she always did that when she couldn't get what she wanted.

'Fine, do we go now?' I was surrounded in less than five seconds.

'Maybe after five o'clock? I've ordered pizza.'

Half an hour later, the doorbell rang.

'Pizzas have arrived,' Jess said.

'Let me get them; I'm starving,' I groaned and headed to the entrance.

As soon as I saw the person at the door, my body froze.

She was not someone that I wanted to see right now.

'What ... Why...' I panicked, not knowing what to say.

Keep calm!

'Hey, Karen.' I flashed a big smile showing all my teeth to my manager, trying to act normal. But guessed I was trying too hard, or my teeth were too shiny. She squinted her eyes as if trying to figure out what I was playing at.

'Are you okay?' She carefully examined my face. 'Are you high?'

'What! No! Drugs are for losers.' I laughed out loud, way too loud. And maybe this was not a time when I should laugh.

'Right...' Karen seemed more concerned.

'So what brings you here?'

'Oh, I want to see Jess.' She said as she moved inside the house.

I stepped in front of her, blocking her way.

'What are you doing?' Karen frowned.

'Um ... Jess is not well.'

'Is she okay? What's wrong with her?' Karen asked. 'I should go inside to check on her.' She tried to walk inside the house. And I once again blocked her from doing so.

'You can't go in,' I said.

'Why?'

'It's contagious.'

'Has she got a fever? I don't mind.' She wanted to move inside again.

'No...'

Hurry! You need to think of something!

'And...?' Karen asked with puzzled eyes.

'Rash!' I shouted.

'Rash?'

'Yes, lots of rash.'

'Where?'

'Huh, everywhere.'

As I was trying to explain, someone shouted from the house.

'What makes you so ... Karen!' Jess walked out shouting to me but was surprised when she saw Karen at the door.

'Jess!' Karen smiled. 'Are you feeling okay?'

Jess stared open-mouthed at me and was obviously befuddled.

'Yes, your rash, how is it?' I asked, patting her shoulder.

'Rash?' Jess asked and gave me a sidelong glance.

I subtly stepped an inch backwards to leave Karen's visual range, surreptitiously nodded my head, and mouthed *Yes* to Jess.

'Can you show me?' Karen asked.

'It's fine,' Jess said and followed with a smile. 'It's gone.'

'Okay, but if it happens again, go to see a doctor and put some cream on.' Karen breathed a sigh of relief.

Jess questioned me through her eyes. I shrugged and acted innocent.

'Come on, let's go inside,' Karen said.

Jess and I exchanged glances – we were both well aware of the third person in the house.

Jess nodded and began to lead the way.

I wanted to grab her arm to stop her, but she'd already gone ahead.

'*Hey*, let's welcome Karen the manager!' Jess suddenly bellowed in the loudest voice she had.

'Why are you shouting?' Karen asked.

'*Look*!' Jess pointed at a painting on the wall. Karen and I both looked. 'Do you like my painting?'

'Yeah, I have one too. Bought it at IKEA.' Karen deadpanned.

'Oh...' She then pointed at the acrylic dog display on the sideboard. 'How about that?'

'Great taste, it was my gift to you last year.' Her forehead creased and she looked confused.

There was a silence.

'How long are we going to stand in the corridor? Can we not go somewhere that has a sofa?' Karen was getting irritated.

Jess nodded and walked very slowly toward the sitting room. Karen and I followed.

I could see the confusion on Karen's face but it was the least of my concerns.

As we entered the sitting room, everything was in the same place as before; the only thing missing was Ryan.

I guessed he heard the shout and hid somewhere.

Karen fell on the sofa and took out some documents from her bag.

'I remember you said you wanted to try something new.' She handed over a folder of paper. Judging by the thickness and from my experience, it looked like some kind of script.

Jess took the script and a smile lifted instantly.

'OMG, you've got me a role in *Run Run Family*?' She was so excited and quickly flipped through the content. 'I've never done acting before, you know?' Her eyes sparkled with excitement.

'While you're taking a read, I will use your bathroom.' Karen rose from the sofa.

'Wait—' I panicked and grabbed her shoulder without thinking. 'Um...' I mumbled as my mind whirled to come up with an excuse to stop her, my manager, the master of my fate, from emptying her bladder.

Karen looked at me puzzled again.

'There's more than one toilet...' She ignored my nonsense and marched into the guest toilet.

I secretly wished and hoped Ryan had not hidden in that toilet.

'Oh, my God,' Karen shouted.

My wish hadn't come true.

Karen ran back to us and pointed at the toilet. 'What the hell is Ryan doing in the toilet?' she asked angrily.

'Peeing?' Jess shrugged, looking innocent.

'He's hiding behind the bath curtain.'

'Taking a shower?'

'He is fully dressed.'

'Thinking about life?'

Karen laughed drily.

Jess and I both fell into silence. In the meantime, Ryan

slowly walked out of the bathroom and came to our side. He checked Karen's face and took a deep breath.

'I—'

'We're dating,' Jess shouted before Ryan could say anything.

'What?' Karen, Ryan and I all shouted in surprise.

Jess saw our shocked faces and she grabbed Ryan's arm.

'Honey, we should come clean.' She flashed an awkward smile to Ryan. I guessed by the twitching corner on her lip, that it was meant to be a seductive smile, yet it was too fake and I almost laughed.

'You two are dating?' Karen asked. 'Since when?'

'Well—'

Jess interrupted Ryan. 'Last month.'

'Oh.' Karen fell silent, as if planning something in her head.

After a while, she looked up at me. 'Did you know this?'

'Um—'

'She just found out today.' Jess jumped into our conversation.

Karen sighed. 'Would you guys like to tell the public? It will be quite cute. Probably raise the popularity of both of you.'

'Well...' Jess became slightly pale; my guess was she didn't expect Karen to go that far. I peeked at Ryan and his face went even darker.

'I could arrange a reporter to follow you guys to pretend an "accidental" leak – you'll look great on the front page. Especially since both of you are releasing albums—'

'Sorry, Karen. I lied.' Ryan removed Jess's hand from his arm. He stepped toward me and grabbed my shoulder. 'Anna is the one that I'm dating.'

Jess and Karen were both shocked as hell but for different reasons.

'Ryan! You will ruin her.' Jess slapped her forehead, irritated.

On the other side, Karen looked at me full of suspicion.

'He is dating you?' she asked. 'You? Seriously?'

'What's that supposed to mean?' I asked.

I understood I was not a nine or ten, but I was at least a six.

'Well...' Karen hesitated. 'I just never thought ... never mind.'

'I love her.' Ryan steadied his gaze on me, making my heart pound faster. 'And I'm serious.'

Karen breathed a long sigh. 'How long have you two been together?' she asked.

'About a year,' Ryan answered.

'Under my eye and I see nothing,' Karen muttered.

'I'm sorry, but—'

'It's fine, I understand.' Karen put her bag on her shoulder. 'I hope you know what you are doing.'

'I know.'

Karen looked at him, and slowly she nodded.

Did that mean she approved of our relationship?

'I need to go now,' she said as she turned to Jess. 'Read the script and tell me tomorrow if you want to take it.'

She left us and walked to the door. I ran after her and stopped her before she grabbed the door knob. 'Please don't tell anyone else.'

She glanced at me. 'I won't, but I hope you two know what you are doing. Especially Ryan – he better not play any games like before.'

The pizza arrived not long after Karen left. We decided to

stay in to watch Netflix because we were all exhausted after that little drama.

On the way home, I had a huge urge to question Ryan about the games that Karen mentioned, but I didn't know where to start. I peeked at him while he focused on driving.

'I'm sorry for breaking your rules,' he said with a mirthless smile.

But I wasn't worried about the rules now; what I cared about was the other thing.

'I can't pretend to be dating other people,' he continued after he got no feedback from me. 'It's not fair to you.'

'Ryan—'

'Anna, I don't care what others think of us. I can give up everything for you.' He slowly pulled the car over to the side of the road. Once he'd stopped the car, he glanced at me. 'The question is, can you?'

The cute young boy was gone; instead, I was looking at a fully grown-up man who knew what he wanted, what he needed. I was the only thing he wanted, the one with whom he wanted to build a family. The enormous amount of love he was giving made me wonder what I had done to capture this precious man.

He didn't know my feelings because I always kept them to myself.

I understood his pain – did he feel he was in a one-way relationship? I knew I wasn't giving as much as he did to me. It hurt me to see him suffer.

'I have nothing to give up, Ryan,' I said. 'I have nothing.' I took a deep breath before I continued. 'I have no family, no parents.'

I looked into his eyes, exposing every true feeling I had,

just to make sure he would never suffer from my absence of response.

'I am an orphan, and Ryan, you are the only person I have.' Slowly, I felt my vision become blurry as if heavy rain had fallen into my eyes. 'I am sorry I didn't tell you earlier, I—'

Before I could finish, Ryan pulled me to his chest, hugging me tight.

'Never admitting it feels like it never happened, right?' He was speaking my mind.

I never wanted to admit I was an orphan; forever denying it made me feel that my parents were still alive, they were just far away.

'But you're not an orphan anymore,' he whispered in my ear. 'Because you have me. From now on, I will be there for you.'

His promise was like a key to my secret door, and it opened up my vulnerable part. I was happy but afraid that one day I might lose him.

※ ※ ※ ※

Never had I felt so good about life. The feeling of loneliness, being abandoned and unloved was like a never-healed wound. Sometimes, just a word or a scene could trigger that pain spot, bringing up all the bad memories and affecting my whole week. But that wound has now become a scar. The weight on my shoulders vanished the day after talking with Ryan.

I felt reborn.

'I should have told you earlier,' I told Ryan at dinner.

'It's hard to bring it up.' He smiled.

'Not for you, you told me the first day we met.'

'Well, I wasn't always like that. In fact, I was like you at first, but my aunt helped me to overcome that.'

'I am glad you have your auntie.'

I guess my voice was filled with envy. Ryan put his palm on mine.

'And you have me.'

Ryan was the man that many girls dream of, and more than that, I knew he was a man that I could rely on.

'You know next Friday's schedule, right?' Ryan asked.

'Yes, an interview in the afternoon and I think you're attending an award ceremony that night too.' I checked my calendar on the phone.

'About that ceremony – would you like to join me?' Ryan's eyes sparkled with excitement.

I think those beautiful blue eyes had cast a spell on me. I answered without thinking. 'Sure.'

It had been a while since I went to an award ceremony; the last time I went was...

My mind froze when I remembered the last one that I went to.

Once again, those olive eyes scrambled my thoughts.

'The sponsor got me a tux...' Ryan mumbled about the clothes he would be wearing. I could tell he was very excited but I didn't understand why because he had been to various music awards before.

'You seem very excited about it.' I laughed.

'Of course, it's the movie awards. I have never been.' Ryan laughed. 'I think I'll see Danny Bale, he's nominated this year. I'm...'

My smile froze, and my mind blanked. Ryan's voice

gradually became muffled like background noise, leaving only the sound of my heartbeat in my ears.

Will he...?
Of course he will, you know him.
But maybe he's away shooting and you won't bump into him.
'Are you okay?' Ryan caressed my cheeks.
I nodded, but I knew my fear had risen again.
No, I am not okay.

CHAPTER FIFTEEN

My goosebumps were up. I felt a burning stare in my back. I turned around, searching for a familiar face, the face that I had been hiding from for two years. I knew he had moved on and I shouldn't worry that he would confront me. Well, he wouldn't care anyway. But the fact that I walked out of our relationship without leaving any hints made me a jerk. It seemed to be a good idea at that time because I knew he wouldn't care and he would move on faster than a blink. But the more I thought of it, the more the feeling of shame rose. By the time I realised it, there was no turning back.

After a good scan of the room, my eyes returned to Ryan. The puzzle in his eyes told me he had been watching me all the way through, even though he was ten feet away from me chatting with an executive director. I guessed my face was overly alert. He mouthed 'Are you okay' to me from across the room. I nodded and pointed to the food bar pretending I was just looking for food. I quickly dashed off to leave his sight and decided to go to the food bar for real. I needed to flush my distressing thoughts down my guts.

I browsed through the hot dishes; there were only small sandwiches and bite-sized food that could fit in your mouth one at a time. I hated them! They were so small and I was hungry enough to eat all of them in one go. But I couldn't do that because this was a movie festival. I was elegant and classy. I couldn't eat like a pig here. I needed to act like a lady and be like one. While I was battling how much I could consume without seeming greedy, a strong scent of custard came to me. I turned my head and saw dishes of apple crumble in small cubes covered with warm custard. They were sitting on the dessert table waiting for my summons. I walked over and beamed at the creamy sauce. The sweet scent of custard melted my heart, and I debated how many of them should I eat. Two were the minimum and four were the max, no, five, or maybe six if I could walk away and come back to pretend to take my first.

A voice flew to my ears and gave me goosebumps. 'Trust me, six is the minimum.'

The stare I received earlier had returned to my back. I wasn't surprised to see him here because I was in his territory, a movie festival. I'd even written my lines so I knew what to say if we met again. But I didn't know until now that I still wasn't prepared to face him.

The owner of the voice continued, ignoring the absence of my response. 'They are good.'

I turned my head and met with the familiar olive-green eyes.

Chris was still handsome and fit; nothing had really changed. His hair was a bit longer and slicked back for tonight's event. The fit of the black suit looked good on him, but the shirt failed to hide his muscular body. I could faintly see the shadow made by the edge of those muscles. The memory of lying on his chest came at the wrong moment.

Wrong.

I bit my bottom lip hard to soothe myself. When I was calm enough, I gazed up to meet his eyes.

'Hi.' I smiled and waited for his next line. But he just stared at me without saying a word. I wasn't prepared for the dead air! I needed to get out of this before Ryan saw the scene. 'I think I will take three for now.' I quickly took a plate, grabbed three puddings and prepared to run.

'Yeah, flee the scene. You're great at that.' His words stapled my feet to the ground. Sarcastic? Was he angry with me?

'It was best for both of us.' I lowered my voice. It was the right thing to do at that time, but guilt came over me as I spoke.

'No, it was only the best for you.' His stern face sent a shiver down my spine.

The sudden change of mood was unexpected. After two years I thought he would have forgotten about it. Probably teased me a bit when we met, but not like this. I didn't have a response line.

'Speechless, huh?' He faked a laugh. 'You can't even speak up for your shit.'

I broke eye contact, wanting to escape his interrogation. I didn't know why the guilt grew over me now. It was the best thing to do at that time. I did nothing wrong, I reminded myself.

A feminine voice softly pierced the air. 'Where have you been?'

A beautiful blonde came to Chris's side. Her hand crooked around on his arm. 'I need you, Chris, they are boring me,' she said as she kissed his cheek. The woman was so tall that she was almost as tall as Chris. Did I mention she was beautiful? Her long blonde hair was tied up like a princess's and her make-up was flawless. Those big blue eyes under the long lashes were so seductive that men would line up just to talk to her. The silver dress she was wearing could only be worn by a size zero woman; the material was so tight and silky that no way could you hide any fat underneath it. I concluded that she must be a supermodel among the top ranks.

'In a minute,' Chris replied as he pulled her hand to his lips. 'I'm chatting with an old friend.'

The woman followed Chris's eyes. 'Oh, sorry.'

She put out her hand and lifted a smile at me. 'Hi, I am Emily Parker.'

'I am Anna Bell.' I reached out for a handshake.

'I hope I didn't interrupt anything?' She smiled.

No, you didn't, please take him away.

'Nope. We were just chatting about our old days.' Chris broadened his smile. His acting was so good I could not tell whether it was real.

'Old days?' Emily asked.

'Anna was my stylist for two years. Her work was ... great.' The genuine smile on his face gave me a cold sweat. I just wanted to get out of this ASAP.

'Damn, I should have asked for a raise.' I flashed him a smile, thinking of an excuse to leave. 'Anyway, it was—'

'So where do you work now?' As if he could see through me, Chris caught me with a question before I could sneak away.

'An event agency.' I didn't know why I avoided giving the real answer.

He frowned after he heard my ridiculous reply.

'Your agency is the contractor for this event?' Emily asked.

It wasn't, yet I nodded because this was my getaway card.

'Yes, I need to get back to work now.' I smiled. 'Great meeting you.' I looked at both of them and fled the scene.

I ran out of the room as the ceremony was about to start. Celebrities and top-level executives were all heading into the theatre. My mobile buzzed and it was Ryan. I told him to go in first and that I would join him soon.

I waited for everyone to be seated and then sneaked into the theatre. The ceremony had started, and the audience was quietly seated and had their focus on the MC. I took a seat close to Ryan and texted him. After he received the message, he scanned the hall and smiled when he saw me.

⭐ ⭐ ⭐ ⭐

Before the end of the ceremony, I quietly sneaked out of the hall. I took a deep breath, trying to calm myself. Watching Ryan receive an award for the movie song was thrilling. When his sweet smile hung on the big screen, the audience including myself screamed like a baby. His thank you speech was short, he expressed his gratitude to his aunt, Magnum and his fans. But when I thought he was about to leave the stage, he stood still and shot his gaze in my direction, searching through the sea of people, and when he laid his eyes on me, a smile rose on his face.

At this moment, the sound of the cheering faded away and the surroundings vanished, leaving Ryan and me, eye to eye. I heard someone's heartbeat like a galloping horse. Was that my own heart beating?

Ryan did not thank me in words, but that sweet smile was better than any speech in the world. Thinking of the life and experience we had together, my joy turned into tears and blurred my sight. I gently wiped them with the corner of my sleeve and dragged my mind to the present time.

The cheering for Ryan didn't stop even after he left the stage. Soon after, the cheering turned into clapping, honouring his achievements. I joined the audience and tried hard to stop the reappearance of my tears.

As the next award was presented, the enthusiasm from the audience wore off. I took a deep breath, trying to calm my excitement. I looked at Ryan, and at the same time, he turned around and locked eyes with me. No words were needed between us; we understood each other, and we lived for each other.

We were both reluctant to look away, but I knew I needed to break it off, otherwise we would be noticed by others. It was good to be in the newspapers, but not on the gossip page.

I pointed my head to the exit indicating to Ryan that I would wait for him outside. He subtly nodded.

I walked out of the hall; people were still inside the theatre because the ceremony was still going on. I walked past some staff and guests who had also left the room but headed to the exit door. I wandered back to the food area, thinking there would be leftovers of those custard tarts. I wasn't disappointed; dozens of the golden morsels were still sitting on the table, waiting for my call. I half ran to them and took a glass of champagne on the way.

'Custard tart and champagne...' I mumbled after tasting both of them.

The softness of the crumble and the sweetness of the custard made the best team. I cherished the food so much that I forgot to pay attention to my surroundings.

'So that's him.'

Did I imagine it? Had a familiar but cold voice resurfaced in my head, or not?

I turned around and was welcomed by a stern face.

Chris was standing just one foot from me. His six-foot-tall frame forced me to look up so I could see his face. The absence of speech raised the pressure between us. I instinctively took a few steps back, just to keep a safe distance. But he moved forward, invading my personal space. I felt a fast pumping beat from my heart, but unlike what I had just felt with Ryan, a mixture of worry and sadness made me nervous right now.

I took a quick scan of the room and felt a load off my mind when I realised there weren't staff or guests around. We weren't attracting attention.

'What do you want?' I lowered my voice trying not to make a scene.

'I saw you crying for him,' he said in a cold and emotionless voice. 'He is the reason you left me?'

The seed of fear grew rapidly, and cold sweat fell down my back, each hair on my skin standing up trying to escape from my flesh.

'No,' I mumbled. 'I met him after we...' I fell silent without finishing the sentence. My conscience prohibited me from saying *broke up* because, strictly speaking, we never did break up.

'After we what, Anna?' Chris asked. Though he lowered

his voice, I could still hear the anger that lingered in his voice.

My mouth went dry and tightness formed in my chest. His intimidating expression scared me to hell. But still, I swallowed my rage and hid my anxious face.

'I met him after we broke up,' I said firmly, without hesitation this time.

There, I said it.

Chris appeared to be surprised. He scratched his chin and sank into his thoughts.

'Really?' He raised his voice, but to a point where it sounded too dramatic, too sarcastic. 'When did that happen?'

'What...' I stuttered. 'What do you mean?'

'I mean when did we break up?' He faked a smile.

I knew what he wanted from me – an answer which I owed him – but this was not the best place or time to do it. While I was trying to think of a way to escape, a few event staff walked past us. They shot us curious gazes and one even turned around to check on us from a distance.

I started to sweat and pant.

'I don't remember, we just broke up one day.' I glanced at the hall door and relaxed a bit when I saw it was still shut tight. I returned my gaze to Chris and his green eyes once again drew me to the memory of our old days. I sighed, feeling guilty for being horrible to him.

'Just let it go,' I said softly. 'We broke up, end of the story.'

'Oh!' Chris chuckled. 'You mean when you disappeared one day and I was assigned a new stylist? That's how we broke up, right?' He dry laughed, and anger was written in his eyes.

A man spoke from behind me. 'Anna?' I recognised the voice and he was the last person I wanted to see right now.

'I think he's asking for you.' Chris pointed behind me.

I slowly turned around and was met with puzzled eyes. Concern, questions, confusion were all written on Ryan's face.

'Hey,' I said in a plain voice, trying to sound natural. 'The awards have finished?'

'No. I was...' He paused, looking as if he was trying to rephrase his sentence. 'I just came out to answer my phone.'

'Cool,' I said.

An awkward silence rose among us. Instead of leaving the scene, Ryan stood still and carefully checked out Chris; he was probably trying to figure out the relationship between me and Chris.

'Hi, Chris Steward.' Chris broke the silence and raised his hand.

Ryan glanced at his hand and slowly reached out for a handshake. 'Ryan Norton.'

Then we fell back into that silence again.

'So, how long have you known each other?' Ryan asked.

Before I could answer, Chris sneered. 'Oh, he didn't know about us?'

'What is he talking about?' Ryan looked at me with puzzlement in his eyes.

The feelings of shame and guilt overwhelmed me. I peeked at Ryan, feeling guilty for hiding this secret from him. I felt shameful for leaving Chris in such an irresponsible way. I wanted to run away.

'Let's go.'

Without giving it further thought, I grabbed Ryan's arm and started to walk away.

'Yeah, run away like you always do.' Chris raised his voice.

I rushed into the car and slammed the door. Chris's accusation had put heat on my face, my heartbeat raced and I felt light-headed and breathless. My mind replayed our past and my despicable actions toward him. Everything Chris had said tonight had stuck in my head, and the memories I had with him flooded my brain. Good or bad, both came like a tsunami.

The olive-green eyes flashed. 'I love you,' he had said.

My mind exploded when those three words popped up. I fought hard to remove those images of his sad eyes, but they kept reappearing. Finally, I surrendered, letting all the memories of Chris jam into my head.

It was all my fault.

I was too focused on thinking about my own problem and didn't notice Ryan had got into the car and started the engine. When the car stopped, I looked up at the strange surroundings, and then realised we had arrived at Ryan's house.

'I know I've broken the rule, but it's kind of late, so maybe we could stay at my place.'

I paid no attention to any rules right now; my priority was to remove Chris from my head.

I nodded and followed Ryan into his home. It was a two-storey house with two bedrooms. I took off my shoes and tiptoed on the dark oak floor. Ryan invited me to the TV room where a huge fireplace with a golden oak finish stood in the corner of the room. The soft-looking leather furniture was waving an invitation to me. I dropped myself on one of the dark brown armchairs and enjoyed the cosy atmosphere.

Ryan disappeared to the kitchen while I was chilling on

the chair. I scanned through the room and my attention was caught by the picture above the fireplace. Ryan's sweet smile shone from the picture and beside him, an older woman had her arm on his shoulders. It was his aunt Christine.

Ryan showed up with two glasses of wine.

I took one of them and poured half down my throat.

'You are thirsty?' Ryan chuckled.

The wine failed to flush my guilt down my gut; instead, an apology speech kept running around in my head. Maybe I needed more wine. Two seconds later, my glass was empty leaving only my lipstick marks. I held my breath for two seconds, waiting for my courage to rise, or for my honesty to take over. I knew there was nothing to lie about or to hide anymore, only to apologise for keeping a secret. My mind drifted away second by second, trying to think of the best opening line, and suddenly, Ryan broke the silence.

'I knew about you and Chris.'

His words were like a bomb that had just exploded in a minefield.

'What do you mean?' I asked, voice quavering.

'You and Chris were a couple. I've known it for a while.'

'How?' My relationship with Chris was so secret that even my ex-manager didn't notice. Ryan couldn't possibly know. This made me worry whether the news had been leaked. I seriously didn't want to be on the front covers.

'You told me.' Ryan laughed. 'Remember when you told me about your work experience?'

'Yes, and I never mentioned him.'

'Exactly.'

I looked at him in puzzlement.

'Before we met, Karen mentioned to me that you had worked with him for two years. So when you told me about your experience but left him out of your list, I figured something had happened between you and him.' He smiled. 'After all, he was not someone you would forget to mention on a CV.'

'But that doesn't mean...'

'The way you kept your distance from me at the beginning...' Ryan trailed off. 'I guessed the relationship had ended badly.'

I was speechless; he had a remarkably agile mind – everything he said was brutally accurate. It was like all my secrets were out, my body exposed; I had nowhere to hide my disgraceful self.

'Good job, Sherlock.' I pulled a wry smile at him.

Our gazes caught but neither of us spoke.

'I'm sorry,' I said. 'I should have told you earlier.'

Ryan looked at his glass of wine, not speaking a word. That was when I realised he hadn't even taken a sip.

'Chris and I—'

'Are you still in love with him?' he questioned.

His sunshine smile vanished, and those innocent blue eyes were lingering with sadness. I'd never seen him so upset.

'Chris and I were over,' I said as I turned my gaze to my empty glass. 'Can I have some more wine?'

I looked up but Ryan didn't come over to collect my glass.

'Please,' I said with a smile, trying to be cute.

Ryan moved his lips, but words seemed to have stuck in his throat. The thought of me driving him away made me sad; the thought of never seeing him again frightened me.

'I left him.' I didn't know where my courage came from, but this would be my final chance to let out the truth; I instinctively believed he would be gone if we ended the day now.

'I know it is not my business, but why?'

I sighed, thinking Ryan might push me out the door any second after I told him the reason.

'At the beginning, things were great between us. But since the day he mistakenly thought I had another boyfriend, our relationship turned bad. He became like a bodyguard, asking my whereabouts all the time. But one day out of the blue, his attitude was as cold as ice. My guess was, my time with him was up.' I hesitated for a second. 'So we broke up.'

'Are you sure you have broken up with him?' Ryan asked.

I looked at him, knowing that he had guessed the truth.

Guilt took over my words and my body. 'You're right, we didn't break up. I just disappeared. I thought that was the best way to end the relationship.' My gaze locked with his, searching for a hint of his feelings. But I could find no emotion on his face, and the thought of him kicking me out weakened me. I wouldn't be pissed if he ended it with me. I would just wish we could have more time before the end of our story.

Ryan lifted his glass of wine and drank it all in one go. Then he came over to take my glass and walked towards the kitchen. 'You need more?' he asked.

I shook my head. 'Just water, please.'

'Okay.' He tilted his head towards the kitchen. 'Come with me.'

I nervously followed him to the kitchen – a huge open area linked to the dining room and divided by a marble island. The minimal design was well equipped.

'You cook?' I never knew he cooked; we always ate out because we never visited each other's home.

'Yes, I like cooking.' He put the wine glass in the dishwasher and took out a clean water glass for me. 'Just water? I have juice too.'

'Water is fine.'

I watched his back, reluctant to lose him. What I had done to Chris was unforgivable, but I wouldn't let it happen with Ryan. It all came down to whether Ryan trusted me not to run away if things didn't work out. We'd just started dating a year ago – was the trust between us strong enough? But the fact that I hadn't come clean and he'd had to find out from Chris himself suggested I was not trustworthy. The fear that he would break up with me was stronger than ever.

Ryan spoke abruptly. 'I dated my ex-assistant.'

Another bomb exploded in my head. 'What?'

He ignored my surprise and continued. 'We dated for a year, and I don't want to lie to you, I loved her. I loved her so much I almost proposed to her.' Ryan took a peek at me.

'So why did you two break up?'

'She didn't love me. She loved the celebrity me.' He pulled a wry smile. 'Karen told me if I wanted to marry her, I would need to give up my career. So I resigned and asked my ex to marry me.' Ryan avoided eye contact, seemingly reluctant to look into my eyes. 'But she said I was nothing to her if I was not Ryan Norton.'

Ryan looked up and our eyes locked; the sorrow in his eyes spelled the end of his story.

'I literally needed to beg Karen to take me back.' He smiled bitterly.

This was probably *the game* that Karen mentioned before.

'Do you still love her?' I asked, trying to search for an

answer in his eyes. But he shook his head before I could get any hint.

'Not since I met you.' His voice was firm and sincere. 'And you?'

Our gaze lingered and neither of us wanted to look away.

'No,' I replied firmly. 'But I still had feelings for him, even after we met.'

Ryan's face darkened, screaming all his disappointment.

I slowly walked towards him and leaned over. 'But your puppy trick won me over,' I whispered in his ear, planting a small kiss on his earlobe.

The next moment happened in a flash.

Ryan landed his lips on mine, kissing me like a burning fire, heating my long-held desire. He dropped his fingers to my chest, hovering on the top button of my shirt.

'No more rule number three, okay?' Ryan said softly.

I laid my head on his shoulder, taking time to calm my desire. But my only thought was me lying naked under Ryan's body.

I dropped my hand onto his belt and slowly unfastened it. But Ryan grabbed my hand and lifted me into the air. 'Bedroom,' he said.

The next second, we were back on the hot kisses and Ryan slowly walked us to his bedroom.

CHAPTER SIXTEEN

'Happy birthday, Anna!'
'Mum! Dad!'
'Make a wish, Anna.'
My palms folded together as I made a wish in my head.
'What did you wish for?' Dad asked.
'I wished...'

I woke up in darkness, tears slowly falling from the corner of my eyes. The dream came back again, reminding me of the happiness I'd once had. The wound had healed but the scar would never fade; I guessed that I needed to carry it forever.

I looked to my side. Ryan was sleeping peacefully; he looked like an angel.

His blue eyes were hiding underneath those long lashes, and his soft lips were shut tightly, which reminded me of those steamy kisses. I leaned forward to kiss his forehead and then carefully left the bed.

It had been a long time since I thought of Dad and Mum; their images had faded year by year. I worried that one day I would forget their faces, leaving gaps in my childhood. I didn't have relatives or friends who could remind me of them, and no one important had lived in my past. I was like an empty bottle.

'Anna.'

The olive eyes flashed in my head.

'I love you.'

His soft lips brushed mine.

Chris was my past; he was important, but fate had led us on separate paths.

The confrontation at the awards ceremony had detonated a bomb in my head. I thought he had forgotten about me, but the anger he directed at me showed otherwise.

Was I wrong? Did I make a mistake? Was he still in love with me?

But did it matter anymore?

'Are you in your dark world again?' A voice whispered in my ear followed by a soft kiss on my shoulder.

I turned around and met Ryan's blue gaze.

'Did I wake you?' I smiled and returned a kiss.

'Yes, your dark thoughts were too loud.' He grinned.

'Sorry, I just had a bad dream.'

'No need to say sorry, it's not your fault.' He kissed me.

His tenderness made me soft and I lost my guard. I became a weak person who needed to lean on others. But I kind of liked that, having someone I could rely on.

'Can I ask you something?' I asked.

'You can ask me anything.'

'Sometimes ... do you forget about your parents?'

Ryan softly stroked my hair. When his fingers touched my face, he gently cupped them into his palm.

'Their voices, their scent, their touch...' Ryan said slowly. I felt his emotion as he spoke. 'Not just sometimes. I kind of forgot every bit of them already.'

This time, I was the one who was stroking his face. The sadness that rose in him made me feel guilty because I was the one who dragged him into my dark thoughts.

'I am sorry, Ryan,' I said. 'I shouldn't—'

'Stop,' he said as he grabbed my hand. 'No need to apologise.'

My hand was then pulled to his lips, and he gently kissed every bit of my flesh.

'I just want you to be happy, even if that means I need to share your pain.' He pulled me towards him and hugged me tight. 'Anna, don't push me away.' He released me and our gazes locked. 'We are made for each other.'

Before I could say anything, his lips met mine, ending our conversation and those dark thoughts with a long steamy kiss.

'What?' Jess shouted in her loudest voice. 'You and Chris?' Her big eyes almost popped out of her face. 'Chris as in Chris Steward, *the* Chris Steward!' Now her mouth was as big as her face; she was beyond surprised.

'Well, yes, *that* Chris Steward.' I flashed her a sheepish smile.

'Oh my God.' Jess was in total shock. 'Why did you never tell me?' Those unbelievable eyes turned sad and disappointed.

'Because I knew you would have this reaction.'

'Oh yes.' She shot me a sarcastic laugh. 'Of course, anyone would have that reaction. It is *the* Chris you're dating.'

'Were,' I reminded her.

'I thought we were friends.' Jess ignored my correction and started weeping, but her acting was terrible. 'I guess I'm the only one who believes in our friendship.' She wiped her imaginary tears with the corner of her shirt.

I knew this exaggerated acting too well. She did it whenever she wanted something. 'Fine, what do you want to know?' I rolled my eyes.

Jess stood up immediately and rushed out of the room.

'Where are you going?' I asked.

'Kitchen, wait a minute.'

I let out a breath, trying to remember what happened a couple of days ago.

My encounter with Chris had turned the week into an emotional roller coaster for me, and talking with Ryan had not been enough to ease my annoyance. Also, I could not tell him everything. Not that I was still in love with Chris or anything, but something between him and me was still unresolved and I wanted to keep Ryan out of it. So I decided to talk with someone whom I could trust, and that was...

'Okay, go!' Jess dropped herself opposite me.

I gave a dry laugh when I saw the bowl of popcorn. 'I'm so lucky to have a friend like you,' I teased.

'Well, I don't always get news this juicy.' She popped the snacks in her mouth. 'You should be proud of yourself – I mean, Chris and Ryan!' She laughed. 'Choose? Why not both?'

'It is not multiple choice. I broke up with Chris a long time ago.' I sent a soft punch to her shoulder.

'Okay, let's hear your story, and I will be the judge.'

I groaned and then began. From the beginning when I first met him until the ceremony, I told Jess everything.

After hearing my story, Jess sank into deep thought. I thought she would deride my immature attitude and lose patience in the middle of my story, but instead, she gave me her full attention without any kind of mocking or teasing.

'Was I wrong?' I asked.

'Well…' Jess licked her fingers after finishing the last piece of popcorn. 'It doesn't matter, does it?'

'If I was wrong, I need to apologise to Chris.'

'Are you sure you want to see him again?'

'What do you mean?'

Jess fell silent, then sighed heavily. 'Unless you want to get back with him.'

'No! Of course not!' I retorted in rage, angry at her for questioning my loyalty to Ryan. 'I'm seeing Ryan now.'

'So if you weren't with Ryan, you would get back with Chris?'

'What? No,' I snarled. I felt heat running up my face and ears. 'It's not about getting back with him – I just don't want to be rude.'

'Right…'

'I—'

Jess stopped me from saying anything further. 'Just forget about Chris.' She patted my shoulder. 'What's done is done. Your apology won't make any difference.'

'But…'

'There is no but. Imagine if Ryan found out that you were meeting Chris, how disappointed he would be.'

The image of the angel boy flashed in my head. I didn't want him to feel sad.

'So...'

'Just forget it and move on,' Jess said. 'Don't destroy your future.'

I hated to admit it, but Jess was right.

I wasn't planning to get back with Chris, and there was no point in being sorry for what had happened.

My future was with Ryan.

⋆ ⋆ ⋆ ⋆

'Number 403!' the fast-food cashier shouted.

I took out my ticket and showed it to him. He took a glimpse and handed over my order. The weight of the plastic bag confirmed that there were two boxes of food.

I was hungry as hell, so I didn't check further whether it was our order.

When I arrived at Ryan's place, he was in the sitting room on the sofa.

'Hey!' I said. 'I have your favourite Chinese food.'

Quickly, I placed the takeaway on the table and got the cutlery from the drawer.

I realised Ryan was still sitting on the sofa. He had his back to me and wasn't moving.

Suddenly a fear rose inside me, and all those scary moments from movies ran through my head. Had he been killed? If I touched him, would he turn into dust?

I slowly walked toward him as a piece of scary music played inside my head, making my emotions spike.

When I got closer to him, I realised he had his wireless earphones on and he was reading a magazine.

I let out a breath, feeling silly.

'Ryan.' I gently tapped him.

He turned around and removed one side of the earphones. 'Oh, you're back.'

'Our dinner is ready.' I smiled.

Ryan didn't rise from the sofa as I expected. He moved his lip but hesitated to speak.

'Something wrong?' I asked.

'Um...' He paused cautiously. 'Nothing.'

Quickly he stood up and threw the magazine onto the coffee table.

'What's for dinner?' he asked as he came over and kissed me.

'Your favourite dim sum.'

'Great.'

While my brain tried to figure out what was bothering him, he frowned after looking inside the food boxes.

'You've brought two boxes of fried rice?'

'What?' I took the packaging from him and checked it myself. 'Oh no, my order got mixed up with the woman before me,' I cried. 'Let me take it back...' I started closing the boxes.

'No, it's fine. Don't bother.' He smiled.

'But...'

'It's fine, let's eat. I'm starving.'

Though I wanted to go back to the restaurant for an exchange, my empty stomach made me agree to Ryan's suggestion.

'Tomorrow we need to drop by Karen's office before we go to the shoot. She has contracts for you to sign...'

Ryan had his head down, staring at his food with a blank face. He seemed to pay no attention to my words.

'Ryan?'

Fortunately, this time he heard his name and looked up at me.

'Yes?'

'Did you ... is something wrong?' I pointed at the rice in front of him. 'Are you sad that it was not dim sum? I can—'

'No, it's fine. I like fried rice.' He smiled and put a spoonful of rice into his mouth. 'So what are we doing tomorrow?' Obviously he hadn't heard me.

I repeated what I had just said and then I added, 'Are you sure you're okay?'

'Sure, why not.' He laughed.

His angel smile warmed my heart and I forgot his weird behaviour.

After dinner, Ryan left the house to get some groceries. I stayed home to put away the dishes.

It had been a long day for me. I dropped my tired body on the sofa after I finished the housework and stared at the blank TV screen. The house was completely quiet; I could hear a humming sound in the background. I turned my neck right to left to relax my muscles. But something on the coffee table caught my attention.

I looked down at the table and saw the gossip magazine that I subscribe to, the one Ryan was reading before dinner.

The face that I once saw every night before sleep was featured on the cover. But this was not shocking news; he was always on the cover page. It was the title that captured my attention:

WHO IS THE MYSTERY WOMAN IN CHRIS STEWARD'S LIFE?

I quickly turned to the story page and read line by line. I almost had a heart attack when I saw the explosive content.

Interviewer: I'm sure every girl is interested to know the type of woman you are looking for.
Chris: Well, I like girls who have a passion for work, are funny but sometimes a bit silly and know the truth of beauty.
Interviewer: Know the truth of beauty?
Chris: It's just my way of saying not overdoing their make-up.
Interviewer: Have you ever met someone with these qualities?
Chris: Once.
Interviewer: Is she your girlfriend?
Chris: Was, we broke up two years ago.
Interviewer: That's sad to hear. Are you two still friends?
Chris: Well, I bumped into her recently, and I do wish we could have more time to catch up.
Interviewer: May I ask if she's in the same industry?
Chris: That I can't tell you.

I wasn't sure if I had read it wrong or if it was the same Chris that I knew. Because never in his career had he discussed his private life with an outsider, not to mention a gossip magazine.

My heart pounded heavily as I remembered the ridiculous lie I told Chris about my hobby.

Did he deliberately do this interview?

Nope, don't be silly, and who do you think you are?

But I broke up with him two years ago, I never overdo my make-up and I read gossip magazines.

He wanted me to see this interview!

My fear rose even higher when I remembered Ryan had read it too.

His weird behaviour earlier now all made sense. He was pissed after reading the interview.

Or maybe I was overthinking the situation, and he was just sad knowing his sign Pisces would have a bad month?

My thoughts were so chaotic that I didn't notice Ryan had returned from the supermarket. I almost jumped when he dropped the bag of groceries on the coffee table.

'Oh sorry, did I scare you?' Ryan came to my side and patted my shoulder.

I had my mouth open, but no words came out. I still didn't know what he had read, and the best thing for me was to take some soundings before making a move.

'Are you...' He peeked down at my hand and steadied his gaze on the magazine that I was holding. We locked eyes, but neither of us said anything.

After a long silence, Ryan let out a heavy breath and flashed a bitter smile. 'I guess someone is still in love with you,' he said.

The truth was now revealed. It was the article on Chris that had upset him.

I grabbed his hand and gave a strong squeeze, hoping that would soothe his concerns.

'We're not sure who he is referring to,' I added to reassure him.

'No, we're pretty sure to whom he is referring.' He pulled away his hand and crossed his arms in front of his chest.

I softly took his hand again. 'But it won't affect us,' I said firmly.

'Anna—' He tilted his head and paused.

I leaned forward and crushed my lips to his, stopping him from saying anything further.

Slowly, I released my kiss. 'I love you, and that's all that matters.'

Our eyes never moved away from each other; it felt like the world was just the two of us, and the trust and love we'd built up were stronger than ever.

Possibly, my feelings synchronised with his, and a smile slowly rose on my angel boy.

'Okay.' He pulled me closer and planted a long steamy kiss on me, ending my long, exhausted day.

⭐ ⭐ ⭐ ⭐

'Tell me you have seen that coverage!' Jess said.

She called yesterday and asked to meet up, which was unusually sudden because she always arranged our meetings in advance.

Usually, we met at her house, but today she wanted to meet at a café. I loved visiting her house because it was big and cosy and very private, but I loved this café more.

'Hey, sweetie.' I held my hand out, waving to a cute creature.

A fluffy brown Pomeranian ran over to me and lifted one of his short front legs in the air. He stuck out his little pink tongue and he looked as if he was smiling. I petted his furry head and he rolled over and showed his belly to me.

'You want a belly rub, huh?' I gently rubbed his belly, and he kept his smiley face.

'Are you listening to me?' Jess asked. 'It was a mistake coming to this café,' she mumbled.

I quickly turned to her. 'No, you did the right thing,' I said. 'Probably the best thing you have ever done.'

Jess threw a ball of paper at me, which landed on the floor. The Pomeranian rolled over and took the ball away to the bin.

'OMG!' Jess screamed. 'Is he our butler?'

We laughed.

The Pomeranian waved his furry tail and walked towards me. He dropped himself on the floor and put his small head on my lap. I gently stroked his head, and it didn't take long for us to hear him snoring.

'So, back to work.' Jess put on a serious face. 'Have you or have you not read that coverage?'

I felt as if I was under interrogation. 'Which coverage are we talking about? You have to be specific.' I acted dumb. Of course I knew what she was referring to, but I didn't want to go over this topic again within two days of doing so with Ryan.

Jess looked at me and mumbled under her breath, 'If this is how you want to play...' She grinned. 'Do you want me to say the title out loud, Anna Bell?' She raised her voice.

'Okay, okay.' I held up my hand to gesture for her to lower her voice. 'No need to shout.'

'So?'

'Yes, I did,' I said.

'He is totally talking about you. Especially the silly part, you are—'

'Hey!' I shouted. 'You are silly, not me.'

'I think the word silly is a bit mild for you—'

'And I think nuts is a good word for you,' I said.

She laughed out loud and woke the Pomeranian, he lifted his head to look at us and realised nothing was going on so he jumped onto my lap and fell back to sleep.

'Does Ryan know?' Jess asked.

'Worse than that, he read the article before I did.' I sighed.

Jess widened her eyes and showed her surprise. 'How did he react?'

I shrugged my shoulders and said, 'He was pretty upset, but I told him it was nothing.' I softly stroked the dog's head. 'And I think he's fine now.'

'How about you?' Jess seemed concerned.

'What about me?'

'Well, how do you feel about this?'

I laughed. 'Are you my psychiatrist now?'

'You must feel something when he says to the world he loves you.'

I lost the ability to talk and speak my mind because I didn't dare to think about it. It would break the China wall I spent months building if I thought I had any, or even a little feeling toward him.

'It doesn't matter anymore,' I said slowly, 'you told me, remember?'

'Yes, but this coverage has changed the situation!'

'What situation?'

'You don't understand?' Jess widened her eyes and raised her voice. I did my palm-down gesture to lower her voice.

She let out a long breath. Slowly, she moved her lips and spelled out the unbelievable words. 'He just declared war,' she said calmly, yet the thrill in her eyes screamed out her excitement.

'War?' I snorted. 'With whom? With me?'

Jess rolled her eyes. 'The interview wasn't only for you to see.' She grabbed my hand. 'He was sending a message to Ryan, telling him he wants to win you back.'

My mind went back to a couple of days ago when Ryan

read that article; he was pissed not because of the interview, but because he knew Chris was challenging him.

'That can't be true.' I wanted to deny her ridiculous thought, but this would make sense of why Ryan seemed defeated that night. My anxiety returned and alerted me like an ambulance siren. 'What should I do?' I asked helplessly.

'Do you want to have another chance with Chris?'

'Jess, I told you—'

Jess interrupted. 'Then you must ignore the article. Do not respond to Chris and act as if nothing has happened.'

'What do you think I was doing?'

The Pomeranian woke up, and within a second he stood up and started barking at something behind me.

I turned around and saw a huge white Samoyed. He looked at me with a smile on his furry face.

'I love this dog café,' I mumbled.

The Samoyed slowly walked toward me, and the tiny Pomeranian rushed up and barked at him squeakily.

I picked up the Pomeranian and passed him to Jess, and I walked toward the Samoyed. 'Hey, sweetie,' I said and put out my hand for him to sniff. After a second, he pressed his head into my palm. I took it as encouragement and started petting him.

His soft fur and smiley face were similar to Snowball's. His furry body reminded me of the night I spent with Snowball alone while Chris stayed at a hotel, angry with me. I remembered the time he stood on two legs to get a treat. Those memories were golden.

I wanted to ask Chris about Snowball, but I knew I'd lost the right to do so. Besides, Snowball might have already forgotten about me.

I petted the Samoyed for a long time until the café owner said it was lunchtime for the dogs.

Immediately all the dogs, including the Pomeranian on Jess's lap, rushed toward the owner and disappeared to the garden.

'What breed is that big one?' Jess asked.

'Samoyed.'

'He is cute.'

'Yes, he is.'

After seeing Jess, I no longer felt calm. I'd put a chain on the door to my feelings for Chris. I could not think or talk about him. Yet the resemblance to Snowball had raised all my memories of the old days.

I went back home at around six and before I dropped onto the sofa, my phone beeped.

A rare and unusual person had messaged me.

> Hey, Anna.

When you're trying to forget about the past, reminders just keep coming back, just as if you're trying to diet but get invited to a pizza party.

> Hey, Derek.

I'd never forgotten hiding my friendship with Derek, which had led to the bad outcome. I decided to tell Ryan tomorrow just in case history repeated itself.

> Free tmr?

> Maybe :)

> Come out to lunch with me tmr, my treat.

> Sure.

After confirming the lunch plan with Derek, I inform Ryan on the phone.

'Who is he?' Ryan asked.

'He's a director. A friend I used to work with,' I said.

'Does he have a job offer for you?' He sounded worried.

'Even if he has, I won't accept.' I laughed. 'I need to follow you around.'

He laughed. 'Like a bodyguard?'

'Yep, I can do martial arts.'

'All right—'

'Wait, you haven't heard the whole story.' But before I spoke further, I hesitated about how much I should tell Ryan because it might link to Chris and I didn't want to upset him.

'Derek had some feelings for me before—'

'*What?*' Ryan raised his voice. 'You are not going to see him.'

'Let me finish.' I soften my voice, trying to calm him. 'I turned him down a long time ago and he knows I only see him as a friend.'

'Then what does he want from you?' Ryan sighed, and the concern in his voice wore off.

'Maybe just as you said, a job offer. We will find out tomorrow.'

Though Ryan was reluctant to let me meet him, he

agreed in the end if I promised to tell him everything after the meet-up.

The next day, I arrived at the café on time. Just like last time, I was escorted to the table and Derek was already sitting there with a cup of coffee.

'You look good,' Derek said. His black eyes sparkled under the light.

'And so do you.' I looked at his arms and shot him an admiring gaze. 'You are like the Hulk now!'

He smiled. 'Yeah, going to the gym a lot these days.'

'Not busy with filmmaking?'

'I've been a bit bored with directing lately, no inspiration. So I kind of work as a producer now.'

'That sounds great.'

'How about you?'

I hesitated, thinking about what to disclose. 'I have changed job. I now work for Magnum.'

'The music company?' Derek's eyes widened and he raised his brows. 'You are a singer or make-up artist?'

'A singer and I have an album coming up called *Derek is a Madman*.' I giggled. 'Of course a make-up artist.'

Derek burst into laughter. 'Can't you sing?'

'If you like the sound of a train running over a pile of wood, then you might like my singing voice.'

Derek laughed.

'So what brings you here today?' I asked.

Derek's laugh slowly died down and he stared fixedly at me.

'I didn't know you had broken up with him,' he said.

I kind of knew he would bring it up, so I wasn't surprised. 'Yeah, two years ago, I found a new job straight away, so it is fine.'

He nodded.

'Did you find out from the gossip magazine?' I squinted my eyes.

He scratched his chin and flashed a sheepish smile. 'Yeah.'

'So that's it?' I laughed. 'You asked me to come all the way here just to ask whether I have broken up with him?'

He giggled. 'Of course not.' He took out a pink envelope from his pocket and handed it over to me.

'Anna Bell' was written on it in beautiful handwriting and it was embossed with elegant flower patterns. My eyes widened in surprise as I pulled out a wedding invitation.

'You're getting married?' I squealed with joy.

Perhaps I was being too loud because people sitting near us shot us odd glances. Derek nodded in embarrassment.

I opened the envelope and when I saw the name of the bride, my jaw dropped.

'Isn't she...'

'Yes, she is my assistant,' he admitted.

I quickly flipped through my memory and, as recalled, she was fairly plain. Not the type I imagined Derek would marry.

'All these years, she's always been by my side. I thought to myself, what else do you want?' Derek smiled. 'So I proposed and she said yes.'

'I am glad for you,' I said sincerely.

Derek moved his lips as if he wanted to say something.

'What?' I snorted. 'Spill it.'

He hesitated. 'How's your personal life?'

I watched his face. 'If you would like to know whether I have a boyfriend, then yes, I am seeing someone now.'

He smiled. 'From work?'

'Yes.'

'Will you bring him to the wedding?'

'Nope.'

'Ah! He's a celebrity.' He laughed.

Nothing could escape his eagle eyes. I hated that he was so smart.

'No comment,' I answered.

'I see why you friend-zoned me.' Derek pretended to sob. 'I'm not famous enough.'

'No, that's not true. You are too good for me, Derek,' I replied.

Derek rolled his eyes.

We continued to chat and share updates on work and personal life like old friends who hadn't met for years.

'I'll see you at my wedding then.' Derek smiled.

'Yep! Looking forward to it,' I said. We hugged each other and both departed.

I went back to work after lunch and Ryan was waiting in the changing room.

'So?' he asked.

I smiled. 'You were wrong – he invited me to his wedding.'

Ryan let out a breath.

'But I still can't believe he is getting married,' I said.

'Why?'

'He is not exactly the marrying type.' I took out the invitation card and read it again. 'Not to mention marrying his assistant.'

'Really? His wife-to-be is his assistant?' Ryan took the card and read it himself. 'It says you can bring one person.' His eyes sparkled with joy.

'Ryan...' I walked over and hugged him. 'You know—'

'Yeah, yeah, I know.' He looked away to stop me from reminding him of our rules.

It made me feel sad seeing him all depressed. I hugged him tighter.

'Have you considered when we're going public?' Ryan asked.

I stared at him blankly because I never thought of it.

'I mean,' he added, 'we can't hide in the closet forever. There will be a point where we tell everyone.'

Was this déjà vu? The same topic with a different person. I couldn't help wondering what if I'd said yes last time. Would we have had a different ending?

Ryan was still waiting for my answer, and as time passed his gaze became clouded with sadness.

'Yes, we will.' I kissed his lips. 'We will.'

Maybe my words or my kiss soothed him; the tightened nerve on his forehead relaxed and Ryan replied with a kiss.

'When?' he asked.

'We will know when the time comes.' I crushed my lips on him, ending our conversation.

CHAPTER SEVENTEEN

I took a final check in my bag to make sure I'd brought enough dog treats because I had a feeling that it would be a puppy date today. Thinking of those wagging tails and big round eyes made me as excited as a child.

A knocking sound came from my front door.

I looked at the clock – Ryan seemed to have arrived an hour early.

Maybe he wants to spend some time together before heading out.

I opened the door and expected to see my sweet sunny boy, but instead, I was greeted by a pair of olive-green eyes.

'Why...' My eyes widened; his sudden appearance blanked out my mind. 'How do you know my address?'

Chris wore a plain black hoodie with the hood up; the shade of the hood made those green eyes sparkle.

'Your manager told me.'

'That's private! How could she—'

'I think she is my fan, so...'

That's true because I remember Karen telling me how good his films were. But still, she can't just...

'Can I come in?' He stumbled into my thoughts.

'Now is not a good time.'

'I just want ten minutes.'

People passed by my house, curious. I reluctantly moved to the side and let him in, just to avoid being in a headline.

He let down his hood as he walked in. This gave me a chance to take a good look at him. He'd slicked back his hair and had the same handsome face, but those tired, haunted eyes erased his usual confidence.

'You look nice,' he said.

I sighed and asked, 'What do you want?'

'I need an answer.'

His determination to get to the bottom of the truth was intimidating.

I let out a long breath. There was nowhere to hide. 'That's ages ago. Why can't you just let go?' I said weakly.

For a second, we locked our gazes, but my conscience made me look away. Every time I thought about or talked to Chris, I felt as if I was betraying Ryan, even though my path with Chris ended long ago. My mind fell into the memory maze again, and the silence between us slowly returned.

Chris pulled me back to reality. 'They assigned another person to me after you left. At first, I thought you were ill or something. I tried to call you and visit your old house, but you were gone. After you'd disappeared for a week, they told me you had resigned.' He sneered. 'That was when I realised you had left me.'

I steadied my sight on the floor, playing with my fingers. But I could feel his olive gaze on me.

'I thought you were tired of dating a celebrity,' he

continued. 'But when I saw you with him at the ceremony...' He chuckled, swamped with self-pity and sarcasm, but that mood gradually turned into rage. 'You were just tired of me, right? Or were you bored dating an actor and want to try a singer this time? What next, Anna? A dancer?' he barked.

Chris's anger made my body shiver, but I wasn't afraid, I was furious. I wanted to let out my frustration and disappointment, uncover his imperfect personality and tell him my true feelings. But when my lips parted, the words never made their way out.

I looked away, ashamed, and I was too weak to fight with him.

'Whatever you say, Chris, it doesn't matter,' I said softly, hoping my voice would soothe him. 'We broke up, just like many other couples.'

'No, I care!' he yelled.

No words could describe his fury; it was even more explosive than our worst fight. I felt cold sweat sliding down my back; we were back to where we were two years ago.

'Tell me,' he insisted.

I took a deep breath to calm my nerves. 'Never a year,' I said calmly as if his anger did not affect me.

'What?' He knitted his brow in confusion.

'You never keep a girlfriend for more than a year.'

'Those were rumours, and it was not true.'

'Even Ben said you change girlfriends all the time.'

His confusion suddenly turned into laughter.

'*What*? You dumped me because of a joke from a kid?'

'You can deny whatever you want, but you had dropped lots of hints to me before I left. You avoided me for months, kept getting secret text messages, returned home so hammered that you couldn't even walk in a straight line,' I huffed. Like fuelling the fire, the memories triggered my anger and it spiked immediately like it had happened yesterday. 'You even held hands with that make-up school woman in front of me, on our anniversary day,' I roared, letting out all the unanswered questions that had once riled me.

Chris stopped sneering and looked down to the floor. Slowly his hand reached into the left pocket of his joggers and he took out a little red box.

'At the family dinner, you said you'd never thought of marrying me.' He played with the red box in his hand. 'But I wanted to try anyway...'

He opened the box and the big diamond ring shone like a star.

'Those mysterious texts and the drunk dinner were the diamond ring dealer. I asked him to find me the best and he did, so I went out and celebrated with him.' He looked at me with the most heartbroken eyes. 'I wasn't avoiding you. I was just...' He paused. 'I worried I would give away my plan before I had the ring, so I thought I'd better not speak at all.'

'And that woman?'

'I thought you liked to teach, and didn't you want to be more well-known in this industry and become an influential make-up artist?'

'That doesn't explain the fact that you needed to hold hands with her.'

Chris looked at me in silence; when I thought he had quit making excuses, he sighed. 'Sometimes, you need to compromise to get what you want,' he said.

'But that's not what I want.' My tears slowly slid down my cheeks like rainfall; I lowered my head and wiped my eyes quietly, hoping not to draw his attention. 'And that's exactly where our problem lies.' I let a breath out, ready to say my last words. 'We were never on the same page.'

'That's not fair,' he said.

I parted my lips, wanting to argue my point, but said nothing. I knew we would only end up squabbling about who was right and who was wrong. When I looked up, my vision locked with his gaze. The tenderness in his eyes once again softened my soul. All the memories scattered in my brain had magically found their way and pieced together, like a movie playing before my eyes. The miscommunication led to our break-up, but the love between us was real and mutual. A sense of sadness slowly grew inside me; the return of a long-gone feeling made me realise Chris still owned a place in my heart. For one second, a thought came to me – what if I opened up more, what if I trusted him, what if...

'I need you.' The tenderness in Chris's voice interrupted my thoughts.

I looked at him with my head filled with tons of *what if*s. Perhaps my puzzled face or my softened expression empowered his next action.

He softly grabbed my shoulder. 'I know you still love me.' He looked into my eyes as if trying to find the answer through my gaze.

I should have said no to shut down the conversation, but instead, I stood there like a doll. Was I buying time to make up my mind or just being nice and waiting for him to calm down? I didn't know. The only fact was I knew there was no turning back.

'It doesn't matter. I left and that was the best for us,' I said.

Chris yelled, 'You thought leaving me was the best for us?'

I thought he would throw a fist at me. But instead, he dropped his hand down to my waist and pulled me to him.

'The best for us,' he said as he lowered his head, 'is to be together.'

He planted his lips on mine, slipping his softness and desire into me.

My hidden feelings found a way to crawl up to my head, showing me all the happy moments of our past. Our first touch, our first hug, our first kiss. Every memory was strong and meaningful, imprinted on my mind for the rest of my life.

My vision blurred, and I fought back the tears, still trying to hide my forbidden feelings.

'I love you,' Chris whispered softly, brushing his lips on mine. The tenderness in his kiss cleared out my sensible mind. My lips had been kissed by him many times but never so eagerly and carefully, as if it was the last time he would ever kiss me.

I moved my hand to his chest, wanting to create a distance and stop his kisses, but I realised my power was lost in his dizzying kiss.

After the long kiss, he reluctantly released my swollen lips. My tears spilled again when I locked with his soft gaze.

'Why are you doing this to me?' I cried. 'Why can't you just let go?'

He tightened his arm around me, hugging me hard. The scent of his woody cologne soothed my mind and slowly stopped my tears.

'You know why,' he said as he crushed his lips on me again.

After Chris had left, I sat on the sofa immobile. My mind replayed the scene over and over again. I never knew anything of his desire and eagerness for me, and now it was killing me.

The thought of going back to Chris appeared and my guilty self tried to flush it away from my mind. This process would take time and soon there was another knock at the door.

'Hey.' Ryan showed up with his usual sunny smile. He looked clean and tidy, his hair was carefully styled, and his shirt was well ironed.

He planted a light kiss on my lips, but the thought of the green eyes came at the wrong time. Guilt, embarrassment, all the negative thoughts I had of myself almost broke me down.

I secretly shook my head behind him, trying to erase what had just happened an hour ago.

But memories stuck tight.

'Are you okay?' Ryan gently wrapped me in his arms. 'Have you been crying? You look—'

'I was watching *The Green Mile*,' I lied. It was probably the first time I had been dishonest with him. But if I told him what had happened, it would just upset both of us. I didn't want the angel boy to be sad. He had done too much for me already.

'Where are we going today?' I changed the subject, hoping he would move his attention away from me. It was difficult to breathe under those concerned gazes.

He winked and shot me a mysterious smile. 'You will find out soon.'

We left the house and got in his car. After a long drive, we arrived at a restaurant next to the Thames.

'We're having dinner?' I asked. But Ryan didn't say a word as he parked.

We got out of the car and by this time, darkness had already embraced the sky, leaving the moon to light up the world. The scent of the river and the cool breeze temporarily wiped away my memories of the day.

Ryan gently took my hand and led me into the restaurant; we walked to its outdoor area, which was decorated with string lights hanging from an open-top roof. The romantic atmosphere immediately warmed my heart. Ryan stood next to a chair and pulled out for me. 'Please take a seat.'

After I made myself comfortable, he went inside the restaurant.

I leaned back in the chair and stared blankly at the river view; my mind secretly dived into that steamy moment from this afternoon. Every word Chris had said today was a reminder of my cruelty and impulsiveness.

Leaving without saying a word, what kind of person does that?

Music rose faintly from inside the restaurant. A guy dressed in a black suit was leisurely playing the violin. I listened to the tune carefully and quickly recognised it was the first song I heard Ryan sing in the studio.

'What...' I was lost for words; the music blanked out my mind.

Slowly, Ryan walked out of the restaurant, holding a huge bouquet of roses.

He smiled as he came over.

'Anna,' he went down on one knee, 'I love you.'

He took out a little red box and opened it to unveil the secret inside.

My eyes widened with overwhelming surprise when I saw a ring with a diamond the size of my fingernail sparkling in the box.

'Will you marry me?'

⋆ ⋆ ⋆ ⋆

It was 5 a.m., and the street was empty and quiet. The absence of sound and breezy cold air soothed the jumbled mess of my mind. I looked at my watch, counting down to my last chance to change my mind. There was no turning back after this. I repeatedly asked myself if this was what I wanted.

This was the best for all of us.

Well, I did the same thing two years ago and it turned out it wasn't the best for us. It didn't do any good to anyone.

Yet, I knew a decision must be made, whether good or bad. It was not fair to either of them.

I looked up to the thirtieth floor of the residential apartments, practising my lines in my head. I no longer wanted to hide my feelings.

My hand lifted in the air, still hesitating before pressing the intercom. But when I pushed the 30/F button, the long beeping sound surprisingly released my stress.

The front door was opened in less than a second. I dashed inside and entered the elevator. It took three minutes to get to 30/F, but it felt like three hours.

A ding sound from the lift reminded me of my arrival at the penthouse, I took a deep breath to calm my nerves. When the lift door opened, Chris was at the front door wearing a soft smile, welcoming me. The black wool jumper and jeans on him looked casual and cosy. His hair was styled and slicked back. Those olive eyes steadied on my face, heating me like a shot of tequila.

My heart pounded so hard; it forbade me from moving any closer. I cleared my throat and straightened my back to give myself the courage to walk inside.

As I set foot in the house, the familiar scent brought back all the long-gone memories. The memories that once belonged to us.

I walked to the sofa, sliding my finger across the soft leather, remembering all the happy moments that happened on this sofa. I looked at the kitchen, thinking of the first time I cooked for Chris, and the bedroom, feeling all the emotion I had when I first spent the night here.

But I realised something was missing from these happy memories.

My eyes fell on Chris. 'Where is he?' I asked.

Chris locked his gaze on me; he waited two minutes before taking a heavy sigh.

I glanced at his sad-looking face, those tears wobbling in his eyes, and the vanished smile.

Every gesture told me a truth that I never expected.

'He's gone,' he said with a quavering voice.

I looked at him blankly, unable to form a single response. A ringing gradually rose in my ears, the pressure in my chest made it difficult to breathe, and a feeling of dizziness crept into my head. I tried to hold together my emotions, but when Snowball's smiley face flashed before my face, I could no longer withhold my tears.

I wept; I sobbed.

Just like my parents, Snowball would forever be in my past.

When I was calmer, I looked at Chris. 'When—' I stopped when my voice cracked.

'Last Christmas.' Chris sniffed quietly.

The sorrow on his face influenced every one of my emotions. My tears were triggered again within a second and ran down my cheeks like heavy rain.

Chris came over and hugged me into his arms. I could feel my sadness travel through our bodies. We no longer needed words to communicate; our feelings and hearts were linked at this moment.

All the happy moments with Snowball flashed before me.

I looked up, realising that Chris was the one who had suffered the most. I lifted my hand and stroked his hair, hoping this could comfort him over the death of his best friend.

'I am not Snowball.' His voice trembled as he spoke. 'No need to pet me.'

I laughed with tears in my eyes.

As our grief subsided, my mind restored sensibility. Quickly I realised the way we stood was far too intimate as a parted pair. I leaned back and pulled myself away from him, but he kept his arm on my back, refusing to move away.

'Chris...' I mumbled. 'Please.'

'Can't we try again?' he begged. 'I can't let go of you.'

'We can't—'

'Why?'

'We broke up a long time ago.'

He sniffed. 'Then why are you here?'

'I want to—'

He stopped my words with his lips. His familiar scent immediately raised a happy memory of us and heated me like a burning match.

'Chris.' I tried to push him away. 'Please listen to me.'

He released my lips to let me talk but was still reluctant to leave my personal space. He moved from my cheek down to my neck and shot kisses on those sensitive areas that he knew too well.

'Chris, you are distracting me.' My voice was so weak that I wondered if he could hear me.

Slowly, Chris paused and locked his eyes with me. 'What do you want to say?'

I looked into his eyes but was lost for words. The speech I had prepared was gone like I had lost my memory. My mouth opened, but nothing came out.

Chris took a step forward, pushing again for my answer. 'Don't you see? We were supposed to be together.'

I let out a long breath. 'No, we ended a long time ago.'

'If that is true, why are you here?'

'I am here to tell you—'

'You are here because you can't let go of me.'

His words left me speechless.

I wanted to fight back, but I'd lost the ability to find the right words to argue. Because he was right, I had never forgotten about him. His face kept coming back like a ghost. Was it just the memories' fault or, in fact, didn't I want to let go of him?

'If you truly love him so much, you should have forgotten me, slapped my face when I kissed you and...' He cupped my face in his palm. 'You wouldn't come all the way here just to tell me you are ending with me.'

He pulled me into his chest and buried his face in my hair. 'You could just text me, and all our past will be buried in the soil, just like nothing happened.'

'No.' I used the last of my rational mind, trying to justify my actions in words. 'I want to end it face to face.'

'Why?' He laughed. 'If you don't love me anymore, why do you care how I feel?'

'Because I still care even though we are no longer together.'

'No, because you wanted to see me no matter what the excuse was.'

'That's a bit arrogant even from you.' I rolled my eyes, trying to cover my mixed feelings of anger and shame. 'If I need to see you, I could just flip through a magazine.'

'I am not in the sex column.' He smirked.

His lousy joke made me laugh, and all my happy memories with him ran like a movie in my head. Our first encounter, first job together, first touch, first kiss ... It had been hot and steamy. Yet, whenever I felt the acceleration of my pulse, it came with undeniable insecurity. My subconscious could never fully relax with him. Perhaps my low self-esteem always made me question his feelings for me. No matter how much love he poured out, I would find ways to deny the fact that I could be loved, that I deserved to be loved. Like being trapped in a vicious circle, my emotions would never find peace if I decided to stay with him.

The realisation shocked me. I guessed seeing him again gave me a better vision of my feelings. The fog was gone.

As if he could read my mind, the spark in Chris's eyes

died down. His usual confidence vanished, and sadness appeared as if a boy had lost his toy.

'You are leaving me, even though you still love me?'

Deep inside, I knew part of me still had feelings for him. I could not control my heart, but I could control my future.

Getting back with Chris would just return me to that never-ending fight and mistrust; we might be attracted to each other but we were not destined to be partners. One day, he will find a better woman who understands him. Time would fix everything.

'I am sorry,' I said.

'Why?'

I let out a long breath. 'Because we are not made for each other,' I said. 'If we were, those misunderstandings would never have happened.'

Chris opened his mouth but said nothing.

After a long silence, he asked, 'Do you love him more?'

Do I? Ryan was like a character in a fantasy, one that was unbelievably attractive and competent; he was also patient and cheerful and could offer the most important things that no other, not even Chris, could give: the sense of security and stability that I longed for. We understood each other like an open book, perhaps because of our tragic history, or simply because we worked well together. Our relationship was like fish and water: they needed each other, they were made for each other. My answer to his question was not simply about my love for Ryan; it was about whether I needed him more.

Suddenly, my stress had magically disappeared. All the weight on my shoulders had gone with the wind because I finally found my answer.

Slowly, I nodded.

Chris took a breath out and forced a smile. 'I see.'

'I'm sorry,' I repeated, feeling sad to see the dispirited look on this face. But there was nothing more that I could do to comfort him, the man that I loved.

Chris didn't say anything, just gave me a nod. He led me to the door. I followed him and secretly took a last peek at the surroundings. The place where I once found happiness and love, all the moments that happened in this luxury flat would become my precious memories, forever captured in my mind.

'Good luck with your new movie,' I said.

Chris narrowed his eyes and looked confused.

'I saw the news in the gossip magazine.' I smiled.

Chris looked at me and slowly lifted an evil smile. 'I'll see you around, you silly girl.'

CHAPTER EIGHTEEN

After I left Chris's flat, I told Ryan everything, everything including the kiss, because he deserved the whole truth. I thought he would be furious and slam the door behind me, but he just hugged me tightly until my lungs ran out of air.

'I thought you were going to break up with me,' Ryan said with his arm tightened around me.

'How could I?' I smiled and dropped small kisses on his cheek. 'You still owe me a puppy date.'

Ryan laughed, returning a long deep kiss on my lips.

His passion made my heart hammer so fast that I had to pull away. I hid my head under his chin, waiting for the flush on my cheeks to wear off, for maybe a minute, or five, it didn't matter. Our long silence was chilling and warm. We knew where our hearts belonged – no more hiding, no more secrets.

Ryan pulled himself backwards. 'Anna, you still haven't given me an answer.'

I looked into his eyes, cherishing the moment. Slowly, I nodded and said, 'Yes.'

His joy went through the roof; he bounced up and down like a child. Then he squeezed my waist and pulled me to his chest.

'But...' I grinned.

As soon as the word *But* was said, Ryan paused and dropped the corner of his lips.

'I have some rules,' I said.

'Again?' he cried. 'Do you want to start a career to become a headmistress?'

'I'm joking.' I laughed. 'But I have one condition.'

'I'm listening.'

'Can we keep it a secret?'

Ryan's jaw dropped, and his eyes widened. 'You don't want to tell everyone?'

'We can tell our close friends and family, Karen as well. But I would rather keep it secret.' I kissed him. 'More privacy will benefit both of us.'

'How about the wedding?'

'How about having a small ceremony at your aunt's restaurant?'

'I love you, Anna, and I would do anything that you wish for. But don't you want a big wedding?' Ryan said. His gaze was fixed on me; love and desire were written all over his face. His feelings were so naked and febrile that they made me feel warm inside.

'Why do I need a big wedding?' I chuckled.

'Isn't that what all girls dream of?' Ryan asked.

I looked at him, and my mind flew through time to the last birthday trip I had with my mum and dad.

Make a wish, Anna.

As if it had happened yesterday, the scene of the tragic accident broke out from my hidden memory and stood before me. But my past would no longer be my scary dream because I had found the key to my happiness.

I cupped my palm to Ryan's face and stood on tiptoe to give him a peck on his lips. 'I already have everything that I dreamt of.' I smiled.

Ryan hugged me tight and returned to me a long, steamy kiss.

EPILOGUE

'Happy birthday, Anna!'

'Mum! Dad!'

'Make a wish, Anna.'

My palms folded together, and I made a wish in my head.

'What did you wish for?' Dad asked.

'I wish there would be a boy that loves me like you love Mum.' I smiled.

Mum and Dad burst into laughter after hearing my answers.

'Of course you will, sweetie.' Mum kissed my cheek. 'And I look forward to meeting him one day.'

ABOUT THE AUTHOR

Juliana Chan, originally from Hong Kong now resides in London with her mother, husband, and beautiful daughter. As a typical executive, she often finds herself drifting off during weekly meetings, letting her mind wander in her little imagination, mostly about eating a giant burger, being a spy, and sometimes trying to escape from the end of the world. In real life, she enjoys watching movies and TV shows, with mystery, crime, and detective genres being her favourites.

Follow her on Facebook and Instagram at @julianachanbooks to get her latest updates.

Printed in Great Britain
by Amazon